The Last April Dancers

Pan Horizons

C S Adler
Binding Ties

Judy Blume
Forever

Bruce Brooks
The Moves Make the Man

Aidan Chambers
Dance on my Grave

Lois Duncan
The Eyes of Karen Connors
Stranger with My Face
I Know What You Did Last
   Summer

Paula Fox
The Moonlight Man

Merrill Joan Gerber
I'm Kissing as Fast as I Can
Also Known as Sadzia! The Belly
   Dancer

Virginia Hamilton
A Little Love

Toeckey Jones
Skindeep

M E Kerr
If I Love You, Am I Trapped
   Forever?
Is That You Miss Blue?
Night Kites
Son of Someone Famous

Norma Klein
Beginner's Love
Breaking Up
It's Not What You Expect
It's Okay if You Don't Love
   Me
Angel Face
Going Backwards

Harry Mazer
I Love You Stupid

Richard Peck
Are You in the House Alone?
Remembering the Good Times
Close Enough to Touch

Sandra Scoppettone
Long Time Between Kisses
Happy Endings Are All Alike

Rosemary Wells
When No One Was Looking
The Man in the Woods

Barbara Wersba
Tunes for a Small Harmonica
Crazy Vanilla
Fat: A Love Story

Patricia Windsor
The Sandman's Eyes
Killing Time

John Maclean
Mac

Jean Thesman
The Last April Dancers

The Last April Dancers

Jean Thesman

PAN HORIZONS

First published in Great Britain 1988 by
William Heinemann Ltd
This edition published 1989 by Pan Books Ltd,
Cavaye Place, London SW10 9PG

9 8 7 6 5 4 3 2 1

© Jean Thesman 1987

ISBN 0 330 30693 6

Printed and bound in Great Britain by
Richard Clay Ltd, Bungay, Suffolk

This is for my husband, Robert Thesman

▣ ONE ▣

DEAR SHEILA
I know about you.
Sincerely,
CAT ST JOHN

"Catherine! Are you coming down for dinner?"

My mother. She only calls me once for dinner, and she always says the same thing. But anyone hearing her voice would think that she had called me ten times.

"Coming!" I shout back as I slip the letter into the top drawer of my desk. I'll never send it, but not just because I don't know Sheila's last name and address. The dismal truth is this — I don't need any more trouble than I've already got.

But if I did send the letter, I'd write much more than I have.

Sheila, I'd say, my father called me by your name last night, and when I asked him who Sheila is, he said that I hadn't heard him right. And then he got that closed-up-tight-and-out-of-business look. He wears that expression the way my mother wears make-up, and I wonder what goes on behind their masks.

I hurry downstairs to the dining room, thinking "cheese" so I'll be smiling when my mother sees me.

"Hello, Cat," my father says. "You were so quiet I didn't know you were home." Tall and weary, he slumps in his chair. His dark hair is rumpled and his shirt seems too big.

Mother fusses around the table, putting serving bowls here and there, straightening place mats and napkins. Her high heels click on the floor. Click-ClickClick.

"Can I help?" I always ask.

She always says "No, thank you, Catherine."

Lately we play lots of games like that.

We eat and I look out the window while my parents talk. Mother talks about her work. She's an estate agent.

My father talks about his garden. That's because he doesn't work any more, not since last October when the electronics company on the east side of Riverford closed.

My father's garden has just started growing, so he doesn't have much to say.

"Do you have homework tonight?" Mother passes me the potatoes even though I haven't finished eating the one on my plate. Her look reminds me that she thinks I'm too thin, too pale, and my blonde hair is too long. I pass the bowl along to my father and look back at the window.

"I've got a biology test tomorrow and a paper for English Lit, but it's almost finished."

I can see Cameron's house from here. The light is already on in his bedroom, so I know he's doing homework. The big pear tree outside his window is beginning to bloom, and the branches spread out like lace against the April sky.

"Then won't you have to get right to work after dinner?" Mother's question is a warning. I glance quickly at her and see her studying her microwaved chicken while she pretends that her question was honest. She really wants to tell me not to go to the old farm with my father again. I look away just as she looks up.

My father stirs restlessly in his chair. "Why now," he begins hesitantly, "I thought Cat and I could take Cameron out to the farm with us this evening. He'll want to see those cherry trees blooming."

In these last few months my father acts as though he needs permission to speak. Sometimes his words drift away and are lost, and then Mother rushes in to finish his thoughts for him. She knows something is wrong, but she pretends that we are the same as we were before he lost his job and couldn't find another.

"The weather report said there might be rain tonight," Mother protests. "I'm sure Cameron's parents don't want him out there getting soaked."

I gobble up the rest of the food on my plate. "Excuse me," I say brightly, gathering up plate, cutlery, and napkin and bolting for the kitchen.

3

Sheila has crossed my mind again. She is like a witch, flickering in and out of my thoughts all day.

The kitchen is clean and neat, reflecting light from all its polished surfaces. I squint. All this shining, sterilized glitter hurts my eyes. Even the water I run over my plate glitters. I slam the dishwasher door.

Sheila, are you eating your dinner now? Are you thinking about my father? He is probably thinking about you.

I lean against the counter, feeling a pain in my heart and certain for a moment that I must be dying.

Last night after dinner my father and I went out to the old farm. We've never lived there — it was Grandfather St John's farm, vacant since his death. Every spring Dad and I go out there to watch the cherry and apple trees bloom. After Cameron moved in behind us, we took him. We sit on the sagging old porch in the April twilight, looking at the trees and listening to the birds.

But last night Cameron couldn't go, and my father was more distracted than usual, so I climbed up the nearest and biggest tree to get away from the sadness. My father didn't seem to notice.

Suddenly I heard him shout, "Sheila! You'll fall!"

He was standing under the tree, his thin face turned up to me, and his panic scared me.

I didn't ask who Sheila was until I was on the ground again.

"You're hearing things," he told me. "Since when does Cat sound like Sheila?"

I'm not dying after all. The pain in my chest leaks away and I hurry to my room, taking the stairs two at a time.

I'll call Cameron, I decide. I'll watch out of my bedroom window and see him cross his room to pick up his phone.

"Cameron," I'll say, "have you noticed that my father is going crazy and no one cares but me?"

I sit down on my bed, holding the phone in my lap, and gape at my perfect bedroom furniture, a gift from my mother after she sold a big house for a big price and got a big commission. White wicker furniture. Everything else is yellow. I feel like a guest.

When the phone rings, it scares me silly. My heart beats so hard it hurts, and I have spots before my eyes. I have to wait a moment before I answer.

Cameron. "Why are you sitting there? What's going on?"

I grip the receiver. "I wish you'd quit looking in my window, Cameron! Don't you have anything else to do but spy on me?"

Where does all the anger come from these days? It gushes out of me and I can't stop it.

Cameron laughs. "Hey, Ms Peeping Tom, you've been spying on me ever since I was ten years old. Now how come you look like a truck just backed over you?"

My vision clears. I see Cameron standing at his window, holding his phone and bending down so he can see me better. He's a head taller than I am, but he's still three months younger. My mother doesn't like that. She doesn't like him growing so good-looking, either.

"Do you want to go out to the farm tonight?" I ask.

"Sure. When?"

"I'll call you when Mom leaves."

"I'll be waiting, Green Eyes."

We hang up and I close my curtains, the signal to Cameron that I need privacy. I move to my desk and open my biology book.

Sheila, who are you that my father calls your name in the orchard instead of mine?

Mother leaves for her office again right after dinner. She'll stay an hour or so, just as she always does, but by that time we'll be gone.

"Bring your heavy jacket, Cat," my father says. He is jingling his car keys nervously. I suppose he is worrying that Mother will come back and catch us behaving like little kids who are running away from home.

With my father behind the wheel, the car lurches up the street and around the corner, one tyre hitting the kerb. "Damn!" His shout surprises even him. "Sorry," he says. "I don't know what's getting into me these days."

I do. He's going crazy. His driving scares me. In a few days I'll be old enough to get my licence, and then

6

I'll drive us out to the farm. I could do it now because I have a learner's permit, but he won't let me.

He hits another kerb at the next corner and swears again. Halfway down the block, directly behind our house, the Fairchild house sits behind a neat hedge. Mother sold them the place when she first went to work. She and Mrs Fairchild do a lot of smiling at each other. Games. My mother worries that I am not interested in what she calls "the right sort of boy-friends." Cameron is too young for me, she means, and she can't get it through her head that he isn't my boyfriend. He's just my friend.

Cameron says that his mother tells him he's not old enough to be interested in anyone yet. Too bad she doesn't know about Cameron and Suzy Karloff. He's old enough.

Dad stops the car two feet out from the kerb and Cameron piles into the back seat, sitting right behind me and putting one big hand on my shoulder. I feel his warmth and want awfully much to turn in my seat and put my arms around him, pulling his shaggy dark head against my chest.

"How are you tonight, Mr St John?" Cameron asks.

The car is moving again, but my father looks over his shoulder at Cameron. "Fine. Just fine. How's everything going with you?"

The car swerves, rights itself, and careers down the street. My father is watching the road now, but his hand thumps on the steering wheel restlessly.

Cameron leans back and talks sport at Dad. I'm not certain Dad is listening, because his hand is still keeping time to his private music, but he says "Sure" and "Yes" at all the right times.

We live on the edge of Waterford, so we're out of town in minutes, hurtling along the road to the bridge that crosses over the gorge. I always cross my fingers when we're on the bridge.

Once, when I was small, my dad stopped the car and walked me over the bridge, lifting me up when we got to the centre so I could see the river crashing along below us. There is a cave down there, deep in the gorge, and that was the first time I ever saw it.

"What's in the dark hole?" I asked Dad. I was scared.

"That's the place where fairies and shooting stars and talking caterpillars are born," he told me. He was smiling, so I knew he believed himself. But I didn't. I knew that the cave was where the dark is born.

Now we roar across the bridge, and I'm glad I can't see the cave from the car. But I'm thinking about it. My fingers are crossed.

It takes about twenty minutes to reach the old farm. Cameron leans forward again and puts his hand on my shoulder, squeezing down. Father is hunched over the wheel, and his hand taps out the beat to his silent music.

I lean my head against Cameron's hand and wish we lived at the farm all alone, he and I. I wish that whatever is going to happen will just happen and be done with, once and for all. Then Cameron and I can . . . what?

I lift my head. We'll be friends forever, that's what. My father will find another job and feel like himself again, and my mother will quit clicking around the house in her high heels and watching me, and Sheila will turn out to be only a slip of Dad's tongue.

But the dark born in the cave is sifting across the eastern sky.

❖ TWO ❖

We turn into the drive leading to the farmhouse, pass the collapsing rail fence that encloses the ragged lawn, and stop by the front porch.

"You kids run around the back," Dad tells us. "I want to check the doors and windows."

The doors and windows are boarded up and have been for most of my life, but my father checks them every time, just in case someone has broken into the house. There's nothing inside but cobwebs and dusty smells. Or maybe my father stores memories there.

Cameron and I race each other around the house, and he wins. We climb up the back steps and sit side by side, without speaking. Below us, stretching out to the pond that we can barely see in the pale evening light, the cherry and apple trees stand in neat rows.

The trees are older than my father. Some of them are half dead, holding stubs of blackened branches up between the living limbs. On the left the cherry trees are blooming, and the evening air is sweet with the scent of them. On the right the stiff branches of the apple trees are covered with tight buds. By the time they bloom, in another week or so, the cherry blossoms will be dying, shedding petals that blow in the wind and settle on the orchard grass.

"How's your dad getting along?" Cameron asks softly.

I shrug.

"Is he still looking for work?"

"Not any more. I told you that. He doesn't even talk about it. There's nothing in Waterford for him. Or in Seattle, either. And Mom doesn't want to move."

"But what about that California job?" Cameron edges a little closer to me, and I want to lean against him.

"Mom doesn't want to leave. And she makes enough money for us to get by. She says something will turn up for Dad pretty soon."

"He could always open up this place and farm it."

I laugh and pull up my knees so that I can rest my head on them. "He doesn't know anything about farming. He's an engineer."

"But he could learn," Cameron proposes. "He must remember how his own father did it."

"Grandpa didn't farm, either. He just lived here.

He wrote history books when he wasn't travelling. My grandmother hated the farm, and when Grandpa died, she moved to the apartment in Seattle."

Cameron is quiet, probably thinking about my grandmother. She doesn't like him.

"You just wait and see," Grandma told Mother last time she came. "That Cameron will end up either living in an asylum or in the gutter. That's the way it is with geniuses. His parents never should have let him skip all those grades."

My mother nodded. Grandma St John has lots of money.

Cameron will graduate from high school a year before I do. Next year he'll be back East going to college, but Grandma won't care about that.

My father joins us, dusting his hands against his trousers. "Everything's secure," he says. You'd think we hadn't been here the night before.

He sits two steps below us and fishes through his pockets for cigarettes. He started smoking again after he lost his job. He lights a bent cigarette, and his hand is shaking. Cameron sees and looks away.

The birds are settling down for the evening, all except the swallows, who still plunge and dart over the orchard. We hear a hawk cry far off on the other side of the pond, and the birds stop their bedtime chatter. The swallows swoop off to the right, where they nest in the old barn. In moments the sky is clear of wings. The farm is so quiet now that I hear my own heart beat.

Cameron stands up. "Let's go down to the pond,"

he says. We edge past my dad and run through the orchard, Cameron on one side of a row of apple trees and I on the other.

"Last one there has to jump in!" Cameron yells.

"First one there has to test the water!" I shout back.

We won't jump into the pond, of course. Not until summer. But we run through the wild grass like deer, and Cameron is first.

We are out of sight of my dad now. Cameron grabs me and swings me around and around until I'm afraid we're both going to fall into the water.

"Quit that, you big jerk!" I yell at him, but I'm laughing.

He lets me down slowly and takes hold of my hand. We look across the pond to the other side, where the mallards nest.

"Hey, Green Eyes, do you want to go and see the ducks?"

I shake my head. "It's getting dark. We ought to go back." But I don't want to return to the porch and my sad, crazy father. I want to stay here with Cameron. And I'm angry.

Sheila twitched across my memory again, as we were running through the orchard.

I worked out this whole fantasy in my French class today. Sheila is really the girl my father wanted to marry, but she died. And then he met Mother, and she was so lighthearted and cheerful and so very beautiful that she was able to heal his wounds. Happy ending, except that he lost his job and went a little bit crazy because he couldn't find another and forgot that Sheila was really dead. Perhaps she died falling out of a tree.

Now if I could just believe all that, everything would be fine.

Cameron and I stroll back towards the house, holding hands until we get close enough to see the angry red glow of my father's cigarette. A lop-sided moon hangs over the trees. I look up at Cameron and catch him looking down at me.

"Cat," he begins.

"What?" I ask.

"Never mind." He trots ahead of me and leans against the side of the porch. "You're going to have a big crop of cherries this summer, Mr St John."

"Why, I believe you're right," my father responds.

"Do you think you'll be hiring kids from the neighbourhood to pick them again?" It's a dumb question. My father always hires neighbourhood kids to pick the cherries, and later on, the apples.

I sit next to my father but not too close, because I'm angry with him for being crazy and angry with Cameron for noticing it and talking too much about stupid things.

"We'd better go home," I say, interrupting their discussion on exactly how many kids Dad should hire in July. July is three months away. By that time the world may have come to an end.

My father stubs out his cigarette in the dirt next to the porch. "Your mother will be wondering where we went," he says foolishly. She knows where we are, and he must remember that. Maybe he doesn't want to think of her waiting for us and pretending that he isn't crazy. He'd rather she waited and worried that we were all dead in a ditch. Then the neighbours wouldn't be whispering about him. They could drop by the house and tell her how sorry they were that we're dead. Dead is socially acceptable. Crazy is not.

Last week my father walked around the block in his bathrobe at seven in the morning, calling our dog. Our dog died last summer. "It just slipped his mind," Mother said to me. "Stop carrying on about it. There's nothing wrong with him. Everyone is absent-minded now and then."

Sometimes I think that she is as crazy as he is. She got that way pretending that nothing is wrong with him.

The drive home is right out of a horror movie. My father's hand beats on the steering wheel, and now he's humming under his breath, but not in time to his hand.

We roar over the bridge and I cross my fingers for luck.

On the other side, my father stops the car by the side of the road.

"I have a terrible headache," he says. He is shaking.

"Let Cat drive for you," Cameron suggests smoothly.

To my astonishment, my father gets out of the car. "Good idea," he says.

I didn't bring my purse, so I don't have my learner's permit. I wonder, as I start the car, what would happen if we were stopped by the police. Would my father explain about his headache? Would they notice that he is crazy?

I ease the car out on the road. Cameron can drive better than I can, but of course he has no licence, not even a learner's permit, so I'm stuck with this. I've never driven after dark before. Nothing looks the same, and cars rush at me from the opposite direction, their headlights blinding me.

"You're doing fine," Cameron says.

"Of course I am, you idiot," I tell him. Behind me, my father is humming to himself again.

This must be a thrill for Cameron. How often does he go for a ride in the country with a crazy man and his soon-to-be crazy daughter?

We get to Cameron's house alive. I slide the car neatly to a stop at the kerb and Cameron hops out.

"Thanks," he says. "I had a great time, as usual." He bends down into the car and for a moment I think he's going to kiss me, but he doesn't. Instead he says good night to my father. Then he slams the door shut and runs up the path to his front door.

I circle around the block to our house. As I drive up, I can see Mother watching out of the living room window. She is wearing her silver satin robe, which goes with her silver satin hair.

I tell my father twice that we're home. He stumbles getting out of the car and falls to his knees. Before I can help him, he leaps up. Under his laughter, I hear tears.

We march into the house, my tall, dark father and little, blonde me. The Silver Lady pounces on us.

"Why are you late? Did something happen?"

My father grins. "Why, we took Cameron out to the farm, Silvie. I told you we would."

"Good night," I say, heading for the stairs.

Behind me, I hear the argument beginning. I bang the bedroom door and walk into my bathroom, banging that door, too.

Here, where I'm safe, I sit down on the tiled floor, still wearing my heavy quilted jacket, and pull a towel off the edge of the tub. I'll cry into it and laugh into it until I feel better. Then I'll go out and read my biology book.

After a while I feel good enough to take a shower, and then, dressed in my pyjamas and robe, I open the curtains and sit at my desk. Across our dark back yards and over the fence, Cameron and I face each other while we do our homework. Every few minutes we look up at each other. Once Cameron says something to me but I can't read his lips.

Over the roof of the Fairchild house a shooting star arcs and fades. No doubt it was born in the cave under the bridge, along with six fairies and two talking caterpillars. And the dark.

Cameron is my shooting star.

In the middle of the night I wake up, suffocating. At

first I can't tell whether or not I'm having a nightmare. Then I hear the humming. My father is out in the garden in the dark.

I hear my mother in the hall, crying. I swing my legs out of bed and start for the door, tripping and swearing aloud so Mother will know I'm coming. But I'm quick to open the door so she can't get away.

"He's out there again," I tell her.

Her face is blotched from crying, and she doesn't look very beautiful now. "Go back to bed," she says.

"You *must* do something," I tell her. "You can't pretend that there's nothing wrong with him. Everyone knows. They all talk about us."

"That is not true! Where do you get ideas like that? No one is talking about us. And nothing is wrong. He's just tired. He doesn't sleep well. It can happen to anyone." She turns away and goes back to the hall window, to watch my lunatic father pacing and humming.

I want to tell her about Sheila. "He thinks Sheila is still alive," I want to say. But I don't, because for all I know, Sheila might still be alive. And important to him.

If we all know about Sheila, then what happens?

I go back to bed and can't sleep. Cameron's window is dark. I wonder what he looks like when he's asleep. He has long dark lashes that shadow his blue eyes. His hair curls around his ears, and he has a small scar on his chin from the time he fell off the fence, climbing over to see me.

A long time later I hear my father coming up the stairs.

"I believe I'll plant peas tomorrow," he tells Mother. Their door shuts.

I fall asleep thinking about Cameron and his girlfriend, Suzy Karloff. I'm miserable, but not as miserable as I'd be if I thought about my parents.

▨ THREE ▨

DEAR SHEILA

*I got a C− for the French test I took
yesterday. I should have been concentrating on
the test instead of thinking about you. Thanks
for nothing. Get out of my life.
Sincerely,*

CAT ST JOHN

I wrote the letter on the back of my French test and filed
it away in my notebook, saving it for the time when I
know where Sheila is. Then I'll send her the test as
proof of how I don't need outsiders popping up in my
life right now.

Suzy Karloff sits in front of me in French. She has
dark hair cut to shoulder length and a short neck, so
that her head seems screwed right onto her body.
Actually, she looks like a fire hydrant wearing a wig.
Thinking mean thoughts about her makes me feel sick.

The bell rings and Suzy turns around. "Are you and
Charlie going to pair up with Cameron and me
tonight? I keep asking Charlie, and he says you haven't
made up your mind yet."

Suzy has an awfully pretty face, and we used to be friends. She still thinks we're friends, which is embarrassing. Every time she calls me or talks to me at school, I think about her and Cameron and wonder how often he kisses her and if that's all they do. And then I don't want to be friends any more.

"I suppose Charlie wants to go, even though he's seen that movie at least twice already," I tell her while I tuck my shirt under my belt and gather up my books.

She looks bewildered. "You and Charlie are still going out tonight, aren't you?"

"Of course we are. We always go to the movies on Friday nights. What else is there to do?"

"Well, you sounded . . . I don't know. Like you didn't want to." She follows me to the door, fidgeting me.

"Are you going to drive or is Charlie?" I ask her.

"I'll drive," she calls after me. I wave and head for my next class, wondering why I ever let myself get into a mess like this to begin with.

Charlie's mother and my mother are friends. That's one reason. And he is what Mother thinks of as a proper boyfriend for me. That means he plays football when he isn't in traction, and he's older than I am by a whole year. And he lives on the other side of town, so he doesn't come by too often. That's the other reason. Mother doesn't like people hanging around staring at my father.

It's April and the sun is shining and today is Friday. I ought to be happy, except for the French test. Next comes the biology test, and I studied for it, so why am I dragging along the hall as though the dentist were waiting for me?

I see Charlie ahead of me, walking with two of his friends. Should I catch up and say hello? No, that would only encourage him. The less I like him, the more he seems to like me. I'm sure that if I told him I never wanted to see him again, he'd ask me to go steady.

Maybe my mother could go steady with him.

This morning when I got up, Mother had already sterilized the kitchen and was attacking the living room. She cleans everything before she leaves for her office, then cleans it all again when she gets home.

"If you leave that, I'll vacuum after school," I told her.

"No, no," she said, rushing at the living room with the vacuum cleaner as if the dust had had babies during the night and would take over the house if she didn't gather it all up within five minutes.

She's always been neat and tidy, but lately I've been half expecting her to start washing the bars of soap in the bathrooms.

In the kitchen, my father was busy adding cream to his coffee.

"How are you, Dad?" I asked. My place was set at the kitchen table, place mat and napkin lined up perfectly. I poured cereal into my bowl and saw that

Dad was adding more cream and stirring his coffee again.

"Well, now," he said, "I feel just fine this morning. How about you, Cat?" He added a little more cream, looked surprised, and then took his cup to the counter and emptied it into the sink.

"I'm fine, too." I looked down at my bowl and wondered how I could eat now.

When I left, he had just poured his third cup of coffee. That time he got it right, so he tasted it.

That's when I decided to telephone Grandma St John from school.

At lunch break I go to the pay phone outside the office and call Grandma in Seattle.

"Hello, Grandma, this is Cat."

"Who?" Her old-lady voice is fussy and annoyed, and I wonder if I got her out of bed.

"Cat. Catherine. Your granddaughter." I look around to see if anyone is listening to this situation comedy.

"Oh. Catherine. Is everything all right?"

How do I answer her question? Of course everything is not all right. But you don't just come out and tell someone her age that her son is behaving peculiarly. She must have noticed on Easter Sunday.

"Well, everything is all right, I guess. But I wondered if I could talk to you about Dad."

"About who?" she asks me, sounding alarmed.

"Dad!" I shout. Now I am getting annoyed as well as embarrassed.

"What's wrong with him?" she shouts back.

"Nothing," I say loudly, looking back over my shoulder. No one is listening. "That is, nothing really. It's just that he seems so tired and . . . absent-minded. I wondered if you noticed when you were here for Easter."

"You called me long distance to tell me your father is tired?" Grandma's voice is getting higher and higher, and I wonder if she's going to scream. "Does your mother know you're calling me? Let me talk to Silvie!"

"I'm calling from school, Grandma," I explain. "Mother is at her office."

"But does she know you're calling me? Why are you trying to upset me? I don't understand."

I lean my forehead against the wall and wish I had saved my money. I could have put the coins in the soft-drink machine and drowned myself in cola.

"Grandma, I just wondered if you had noticed how tired Dad seems. I only wondered if maybe you might come over and talk to him. After all, you're his mother . . ."

"I don't know what you're talking about, Catherine, but you may be sure that I'm going to have a chat with Silvie about this. I can't have people calling me up and making no sense whatsoever. I'm not well enough for all this childish nonsense. When I was your age, I didn't call my grandmother from school, sneaking around behind my mother's back."

"Good-bye, Grandma. I'm sorry I bothered you."

I hang up, my face burning.

A hand squeezes my shoulder. I look up, startled. "You had lunch yet, Green Eyes?" Cameron asks.

"No." I hope he doesn't ask me to explain the phone call. I don't want him to learn that all the St Johns are more or less demented these days.

"Let's go, then. The line is a mile long already." He steers me down the hall, his hand on my elbow, and for some reason he starts grinning.

"I talked to Suzy," I say, and he stops grinning. Serves him right. "She's going to drive tonight. If you see Charlie before I do, will you tell him?"

Cameron doesn't like Charlie, but Charlie is too simple-minded to know. Cameron will have to work hard to be polite. Good. If I'm not happy, why should he be?

"Why do you go out with that jerk?" he asks. "You could date anyone. Charlie is such a cretin."

"My mother doesn't think so," I tell him.

"Your father thinks he's a dipstick."

"He's hardly in any shape to judge, is he?" I blurt without thinking.

Cameron squeezes my arm again. "Come on, Cat. That was dumb."

We go through the lunch line together, not speaking. I'm not hungry, but I pick up a sandwich and a carton of milk.

The cafeteria is crowded, and we can't find seats where we usually sit. Cameron steers me towards a back corner.

We've hardly begun to eat when Mary Beth Ogden slips into the seat next to me. "I've been trying to catch up with you all day."

"Hey!" I say. "You've changed your hair." Mary Beth's dark blonde hair is pulled back from her face, somewhat like mine.

"Never mind my hair. I've got a catastrophe on my hands. Won't you come back on the dance committee?"

Cameron stares at me. "I didn't know you left the committee," he says. "Why?"

"Too busy or something," Mary Beth tells him, as though I'm not here. "But we need her back, at least for the spring dance. Sherie is going to have her tonsils out and nobody else can do the decorations right except Cat."

"Cat's too busy," I say coldly. "She told me that herself."

Mary Beth gawks at me and then laughs. "Sorry, Cat!"

I can't stay annoyed at Mary Beth, so I grin at her. "But I can't come back. I really am too busy."

"Busy with what?" Cameron asks me.

"This conversation is none of your business," I tell him. "Eat your lunch and leave us alone."

Cameron gets up and moves down two places. "Carry on," he says, and I can see the laughter deep in his eyes. I turn my back on him.

"Please," Mary Beth begs. "Just for the spring dance. If you could help us out I'll love you forever."

"A week from tomorrow, right?"

"Right. Will you do it?"

I bite into my sandwich to give me time to think up an excuse. Chewing doesn't activate my brain, so I'm stuck with the awful truth. "I really don't want to do it, Mary Beth. That's my birthday, and I wasn't even planning on going to the dance."

"Well, you don't have to go. Just help with the decorations."

That means working in the school gym two afternoons before the dance and most of that Saturday morning. I'd be away from home. Dad would be by himself even longer than usual. And Saturdays are awful anyway, with Mother showing houses from morning until dark.

"Absolutely no, Mary Beth. I'm sorry."

She blinks and her cheeks turn pink. Mary Beth is sensitive and good and one of my favourite people in all the world, and I am hurting her feelings because I don't explain.

"Cat," she says finally, "is something wrong?"

I taste my milk. "Why do you ask that?"

"Lately . . ." she begins. I look at my sandwich and she looks at the wall. We both wait for her to say that lately I've been rotten. She doesn't, however.

"If you should change your mind, call me," she says as she stands up. "Call me anyway, even if you don't change your mind. We haven't had a good talk in ages."

"I'll do that." But I won't call her. I haven't been

calling anyone lately, except Cameron. I'm afraid that I'll start talking and not be able to stop, and everything that I'm thinking will come pouring out of my mouth.

When she leaves, Cameron comes back. "I thought you'd be going to the spring dance," he says. "You and Charlie. It's so romantic."

I glare at him. He's laughing at me again. "The dance is on my birthday. I don't want to go then."

"What are you going to do to celebrate?" he asks.

"We're going to have a family thing. Grandma might be coming for the weekend."

He catches me in my lie. "You don't have any plans. You're hiding out. Listen, I'll spend your birthday with you. We'll do something different. Maybe an all-day picnic and then Seattle for dinner and a movie. Would you like that?"

Cameron is asking me for a real date. My hands are ice.

"Aren't you taking Suzy to the spring dance?"

He shakes his head.

"You'll hurt her feelings," I say.

"She's going to Portland to see her brother," Cameron says as he scrapes his plate carefully and pops the last of his spaghetti into his mouth.

So that's it. For a moment, I really thought something had happened between us. I push my unfinished sandwich away.

"I can't spend the whole day away from Dad," I say. "It's a great idea, though."

Two boys from Cameron's maths class rush up and

he turns away to talk to them, leaving me to sort out my feelings. Part of me shivers from the pleasure of his invitation, and part of me is furious that I was his second choice for a date. And underneath it all, I'm angry with my father.

Or maybe I'm angry with myself because I appointed myself his watchdog. For weeks I've hung around the house on Saturdays and Sundays. It's as if I'm waiting for something to happen. Or maybe I'm afraid that something will happen if I'm not there.

Cameron's friends leave just as the bell rings. He turns to me.

"Why don't we take your dad with us? You could drive! You get your licence that day."

I'd forgotten about that. Would Dad let me drive all the way to Seattle if I had my driving licence? I couldn't stand the trip if he were driving.

"I'll talk to Dad about it," I say as we carry our trays back to the racks.

"But if he doesn't want to come, you'll come without him?" Cameron urges. "He could stay by himself for one day."

"I have to run," I tell him, and I turn away and hurry up the stairs toward my next class.

Sheila, I think, why don't you stay with my father for one day so I can spend it with Cameron?

Or better yet, why can't my own mother spend one Saturday at home?

I pass Mary Beth in the hall and smile at her. "Call me!" she says and I nod.

I know why Mother always works on Saturdays. If she stayed home, she couldn't play her games any more. She couldn't pretend there's nothing wrong with my father.

◼ FOUR ◼

"I put the peas in today," my father tells me.

We are standing together on the patio in the weak afternoon sunshine, and he is pointing to the fence on the south side of the garden. A thin line of fresh dirt shows at the base of the fence. Even in the middle of summer that little strip of the garden is always shadowed by the tall fence. The peas won't grow.

"That's great, Dad. What else did you do today?"

"Why, now, let me think." He sits down on the bench and pulls out his cigarettes. I see that he cut himself shaving today. And his old gardening shoes have been shined. He notices his shoes at the same moment I do.

"It looks like I shined my shoes." He laughs.

Half an hour later, in my room, I discover that I lost

my pencil sometime during the day, and I don't have another, so I run downstairs to my father's study to get one. Dad is still outside — I see him through the study window.

For a moment I stand there and watch him looking at his little garden. The rows run straight for a few feet and then stagger in all directions. While he was putting in the lettuce and radish seeds, he discovered that he had more seeds than he thought, so when he ran out of prepared space, he scratched little ditches frantically, pouring in seeds and cursing himself under his breath. Now the seeds have sprouted into a little marching army, but some of the soldiers are deserting into the grass in confusion.

I can't bear the bewildered expression on his face, so I look down at his desk, hoping to see a pencil in the mess of papers and junk mail scattered there. Instead, I see a letter, right on top and only half finished, as if Dad had been interrupted in the midst of it.

MY DEAREST SHEILA
I find myself thinking about you during the terrible times. It's almost as if I turn back the pages of a book and concentrate on a peaceful chapter . . .

I put the letter down and go back to my room without a pencil. I have a lump in my throat.

At dinner that night Mother asks me if I'm going out.

"Charlie's taking me to a movie. We always see movies on Friday nights."

She nods. "You like Charlie, don't you?" She's busy with her salad and doesn't see the look on my father's face.

"He's all right," I say, exchanging smiles with Dad.

"His parents are lovely people," Mother goes on.

"Yes," I tell her. Actually, I hardly know Charlie's parents and hope I never know them any better. They are like the people in magazine advertisements. Glossy and stiff, with big fake smiles. "What are you two planning tonight?"

Dad says, "Well, now, I thought I'd just drop by the farm and see how the fruit trees are doing."

I shouldn't have asked. For a long time now Mother goes back to the office for an hour or so after dinner, and Father goes to the farm. When they get home they watch TV and then go to bed.

Things used to be different. They played cards on Fridays with other couples or went out to dinner. Sometimes they had small parties. But all that changed.

We finish eating in silence.

Both my parents are gone when Suzy stops by the house for me. Charlie and Cameron are already in the car, Cameron in front with Suzy. I get into the back with Charlie.

"Sorry we're late," Charlie says, slinging his arm around my shoulders.

"It's my fault," Suzy tells me. "I lost track of the time. You must have been wondering what happened to us."

No, I hadn't been wondering. I was standing in my

33

father's study, looking out at his crazy garden. The letter to Sheila was gone. As soon as my parents left, I went straight to the study, but I couldn't find it in the mess on top of his desk or in any of his drawers.

I did find Grandpa St John's watch in the top drawer. It was ticking, and the silver case had been polished. For as long as I can remember, that old round watch had been tucked away in the bottom drawer of Father's desk.

I opened the watch cover and saw the minute hand move with a little jerk from one thin mark to another. That's a minute you won't get back, Cat, I told myself. None of us will. It's gone forever.

I love movies, even bad ones, but we were late getting here and our seats are the awful ones down at the front, with the screen looming over us.

Charlie leans close and whispers in my ear. "I wish you'd change your mind about the dance."

"Hush," I tell him. "I want to see the movie."

I can smell Charlie's aftershave. His reddish-brown hair looks just cut, and he's wearing his best jacket and a white shirt, while the rest of us are in jeans and sweaters. I know it's not his birthday, so I lean back in my seat, wondering what's going on.

Charlie reaches for my hand and squeezes it. "I wish I had my car," he mutters in my ear.

I push his hand away. Now I'm certain why Charlie dressed up. His mother has been after him again, so he's going to start off again about what he calls "our relationship." When Suzy takes me home, Charlie will get out, too, and follow me into the house. We'll end up having another wrestling match in the kitchen, with Charlie trying to kiss me while I try to escape his long arms.

"Please," Charlie whispers. "Won't you go to the dance with me? Your folks will understand. You can celebrate your birthday the next day or the day before. Or something."

"Quiet!" the man behind us says loudly. "You wanna propose to the girl, wait till the movie's over."

Everyone laughs, including Cameron. Charlie slouches in his seat. Good. Maybe now he'll shut up and let me watch the movie.

When the lights go on, I see that Suzy and Cameron are holding hands, and I have to look away. I let Charlie take my hand then.

To Charlie's disgust, my parents are still up when we get back to my house. Every light on the ground floor is on.

"I could come in, I guess, and say hello to your folks," Charlie says. "Why do you suppose they're still up? It's almost midnight."

"Maybe they have company," Cameron says.

I know they don't. My parents' cars are the only ones in the drive, but I take advantage of Cameron's idea.

"It's probably the Shelby's," I say. "Good night, everybody. I had a great time." I squeeze out of the back seat and slam the door shut before Charlie can follow me.

Suzy waits until I get up on the porch, then honks once and drives away.

My father is sitting alone in the living room, watching television.

"Has Mom gone to bed?" I ask.

My father does not answer. He leans forward, elbows on knees, and stares at the screen. His fingers are laced together in a tight knot. He is watching an old gangster movie, one that I know he's seen before.

I move quietly around the house turning out lights, until my father sits under the only lamp still burning.

"Good night, Dad."

"Good night, Sheila."

I stop right where I am. "It's me, Cat," I tell him.

He looks up, smiling. "Why, now, so it is. Did you have a nice time, Cat?"

"I had a very nice time, Dad."

I close the curtains in my room before I turn on the light. I don't want to take the chance of looking out of my window, seeing Cameron's window dark and knowing for certain that he's still with Suzy. This way, I don't have to know anything I don't want to know.

Before Mother replaced everything in my room I could relax here, but now I must try to live up to the furniture. That means I hang up my clothes as soon as I take them off.

I put on my bathrobe and carry a clean nightgown into my bathroom, strip down, and throw my underwear in my bin. After I pin up my hair, I take a quick shower, and I am careful not to think about anything at all.

I have been very careful lately, my mother cleans everything in sight, and my father is crazy. We are a dandy bunch.

Back in my room, I find that I can't stand all that closed-in perfection. There isn't enough air in here!

Now I don't care whether Cameron is home or not. I yank back the curtains and open the window, gulping in air.

Cameron is home. He is standing in his window, with the light behind him. He is looking at my window.

I bend down and turn on my small desk lamp.

Cameron raises one hand in greeting, then holds the telephone up for me to see. I dial his number.

"Cat," he says.

"I didn't know you were home," I whisper.

"My folks aren't home. I'll help you over the fence if you come to my place for a while."

"My dad is still up. He'd see me leave."

"Go out your window and across the porch roof, the way you used to," Cameron says quickly, his voice rough with excitement.

What are we doing? We are out of our minds.

"Okay," I whisper and hang up the phone.

I'm about to close the curtains again when I wonder why I bother. Cameron has seen me in a nightgown before. What difference does it make? Oddly, I know that it makes a big difference now. I pull up the skirt of my nightgown and swing my legs over the windowsill. I see Cameron crawling out of his window, too, reaching for the branches of the pear tree. He could just let himself out the front door, but I understand why he doesn't.

The wooden tiles are rough under my bare feet and wicked with splinters. I creep up to the edge and sit down, resting my toes on the top of the brick wall that extends to the edge of the patio. I slip off the edge of the roof, balancing myself on the top of the wall, holding my arms out and wobbling a little. I'm cold and I don't care.

At the end of the wall I jump down to a planter and then to the ground. Cameron, a dark shape on the fence, beckons to me.

The grass is slick and wet under my feet as I run to the woodpile Dad stacked against the back fence. Cameron reaches a hand to me when I get to the top of the woodpile and pulls me up. Just as I step to the top of the fence, he jumps lightly down on the other side, and I follow, knowing he will catch me. He always does.

He doesn't let go of me.

"Cat," he whispers. "My green-eyed Cat."

I feel his arms around me, pulling me against him, and I touch his face before I wind my arms around his neck.

We stand like that, not kissing, not talking, just standing. I hear his heart beat. He grabs my long hair and pulls my head back while he studies my face.

When he finally speaks, his voice is so hoarse I can hardly understand him.

"I've got Cracker Jacks in my room. You want a box?"

He grins suddenly and I burst out laughing.

"Shh. Stop." He pulls my face against his shoulder. "Don't wake up the neighbours."

"Do you really have Cracker Jacks in your room?" I whisper.

"Don't I always? Why else would you have made all those midnight trips to my bedroom when you were twelve?"

He's just goofing around again, not realizing that what he thinks is a joke is hurting me.

"Can we please go through the house rather than up the tree?" I ask, pulling away from him. I'm remembering my nightgown, suddenly. And I'm remembering that I'm nearly sixteen years old.

"Sure." He walks beside me across the dark yard and opens his kitchen door.

His kitchen smells of bread and chocolate, rather than disinfectant. I inhale as we walk through it, wishing our kitchen smelled as if people lived in the house instead of machines.

He does have Cracker Jacks in his room. And glasses of cola clinking with ice cubes. He knew I'd come.

We sit side by side on the floor, the only place in the room where there's enough space except for his bed. All the chairs are heaped with piano music, books, records, clothes, and trash. His room looks the way mine used to, before the wicker furniture came.

"Here's to Suzy and Charlie," he says, lifting his glass. "Did you know they're sneaking around on us?"

I cough through a mouthful of cola.

"It's true," he says. "We have been betrayed."

I begin laughing. I've spilled Cracker Jacks all over my lap. "You're dreaming, Cameron. I think Charlie was going to ask me to go steady tonight."

"I think he was, too. His mother thinks that it's a good idea. So does my mother."

"And so does mine. But why would he ask me to go steady if he's sneaking around with Suzy?"

"She is his mad passion." Cameron's dark blue eyes hold mine.

I shake my head. "I don't believe you."

"He promised his mother that he'd take you to the senior prom, and she promised your mother. It's all set. But he hungers for the fair Suzy."

"And you're taking her to the prom," I say flatly. Charlie and I hadn't discussed the prom yet. I'd planned on turning him down if he asked me, even though I was sure Cameron wouldn't ask me. Because, of course, he'd be going with Suzy.

"No, I am most definitely not taking her to the prom. A little honesty is what's called for right about now. Charlie and Suzy are made for each other. What do you think?"

How is it that suddenly I don't seem to understand anything that's going on in my life? Haven't I been paying attention? "It's all okay with me," I say finally. "I'm just surprised, that's all. How did you find all this out?"

"Suzy confides her most secret thoughts to Angela DiSalvo, who tells all to her steady boyfriend —"

"Who talks too much," I say. "Does everyone in town know what's going on except me?"

Cameron leans back against the bed. "All except thee and me, until this afternoon, that is."

I eat my Cracker Jacks. "Hmm. I guess I ought to be devastated or something."

"Don't exert yourself. I was pretty sure you could handle the news."

I look back at him. "You don't seem very broken up."

He grins again, and a star shoots across my mind, dazzling me.

"I can live with it. Let's talk about your birthday."

I'm ready, but just then I hear the front door open. "Your folks!" I gasp.

Cameron puts his finger to his lips and gestures toward his window. I repress the urge to giggle. This is ridiculous. Cat St John is going to crawl out of a boy's window in the middle of the night. Wearing a nightgown.

Cameron helps me from the windowsill to the tree and guides me as I step down from branch to branch. When my nightgown catches, Cameron pulls it loose before what is left of my dignity is gone.

I cling to the last branch, uncertain. Cameron

drops to the ground lightly, then reaches up for me. Hand in hand we run away from the house. Rooms are lighting up one by one and then going dark, as his parents lock up for the night. He bunks me up to the top of the fence and I swing over to the woodpile.

"Good night," he whispers, his face close to the fence.

On the other side I lean my head against the rough wood for a second. "Good night."

I pull myself up on the brick wall again. The hardest part is going up the slope of the porch roof. I never told Cameron that this scares me. I'm out of breath, more from fright than hurrying, and when I touch my windowsill at last, I'm so relieved that I'm giddy. I don't feel really safe until I'm inside.

I wave to Cameron, who is standing at his window, watching. His light goes out.

❋ FIVE ❋

"I want to see her right now!"

My eyes snap open like window blinds. It's morning and Grandma St John's voice slices through my sleep.

"Catherine!"

Grandma St John looms in my doorway like a wicked witch. Her usually perfect hair is frizzled like a stainless steel scouring pad; her fat face is so red it could glow in the dark. Behind her, Mother gestures helplessly.

"Grandma?" I get out of bed, numb with surprise, and grope for my robe.

"Your grandmother came from Seattle to talk to you this morning," Mother says, as if she were announcing a scientific breakthrough.

I don't need to ask why Grandma is here. That stupid phone call of mine could go down in history as an example of humanity's uncontrollable desire to self-destruct.

Grandma advances on me like an avalanche.

"I hope you have some idea of how much you have upset me," she cries. I notice that she is not so upset that she forgot to put on half of her jewellery. She raises a hand wearing three diamond rings and presses her fingers against her eyes. "I haven't had a moment's peace since you called."

Mother helps Grandma sit down in my white wicker rocker and settles herself on the small chair at my desk.

"Will you please explain this phone call to me, Catherine," Mother says patiently.

I am struggling to get my arms into the sleeves of my robe — I'll feel vulnerable until I get myself zipped inside several yards of velour. "Where's Dad?" I ask. I don't want him to hear the battle I know is about to begin.

"Your father has gone for a walk," Mother says.

"He didn't want to face his own mother," Grandma bleats.

"But we didn't know you were coming. Why didn't you call us? I could have fixed you a really nice breakfast —"

"Oh, Silvie, will you shut up?" Grandma exclaims. "You do go on so." She fixes her faded blue eyes on me.

"Grandma," I begin.

"I can't have it," she cries. "I can't have any more phone calls about Richard. God knows I did my best, but some children don't appreciate anything."

"What are you talking about?" I ask, bewildered. How did appreciation get into this? For the first time the thought occurs to me that a mother like her could be a lifetime blight.

"I wish," Mother says plaintively, "that we could begin from the beginning. I really don't know what is going on here, and I have to show a house in forty-five minutes."

"Are you talking to me, Silvie?" Grandma snaps. "Are you asking me to explain this? It was your daughter who called me and told me that my son is acting like a lunatic —"

"I did not!" I scream. "I never said that!"

I am furious now, for I can see that Grandma has noticed Dad's behaviour. I never said he was acting like a lunatic. She must think he is or she wouldn't have put it that way.

"My God," Mother says. She is staring at me as if I were a louse. "Is that what you told your grandmother? How could you have done something like that?"

Looneyville. We are all crazy. We are arguing about what I didn't say so that we can avoid the real problem.

I draw a deep breath, determined to control my temper. "Why don't we get right down to facts, since we're all gathered together in one room?"

"I won't tolerate sarcasm, miss," Mother says.

Stubbornly I plough on. "Dad is sick. Something is wrong with him, and pretending that everything is fine won't help him. Does he need a doctor? Is he having some sort of breakdown? Does he need a shrink?"

"A *what*?" Grandma yells. "A *what*?"

"She means a psychiatrist," Mom supplies.

"I know what she means and I won't stand for it. Richard's brother never needed a psychiatrist, God rest his soul. He went out and made money—he didn't hang around the house talking to himself and forgetting names and going on and on about that old farm that should have been left to me and not Richard!"

Grandma collapses against the back of the rocker, out of breath and gasping for air. I look at Mother for some sort of response.

Mother bends her silver head and plucks at a pleat in her skirt. "Catherine, how could you?" she whispers.

Grandma glares at me. "Well? What are you going to do about this?" she demands. "Are you just going to sit there as if it's all right to frighten an old woman to death about her only living son? Are you trying to kill me, Catherine?"

I can't believe any of this. Maybe I'm dreaming. Somehow I have become guilty of something—I'm not sure what—and now we can all pretend that I'm the only one with problems.

"Look," I say, "are we going to talk about Dad or not? Doesn't anyone care but me? You must see that he's sick. Everyone sees it."

Mother shakes her head. "He is only tired. I told you that. All this job-hunting has worn him out. You're such a child —"

"He hasn't looked for a job for a month!" I break in. "He's too sick to look for a job. When he talks, half the time he doesn't make any sense at all. How can he look for work when he's like this?"

"His brother James always worked," Grandma says. She is digging through her purse, and I wonder idiotically if she is going to pull out Uncle James's old employment records just to prove her point. She pulls out a handkerchief instead and dabs at her nose. "He went to work the day he graduated from college and worked until the day he died." She bursts into tears and bends over her lap, hugging her purse to her chest. "I wish *I* had died the day Leah buried him after that tacky funeral."

I am horrified now. I remember Uncle James only slightly, since I was six when he died, but I remember vividly how Grandma grieved.

Mother goes to Grandma and kneels beside her chair. "I'll fix you some tea. Would you like that? A little tea and perhaps a bit of toast?"

Grandma raises her head. "I'd rather have muffins and jam," she sniffs.

I swallow my crazy laughter until they wobble out of the room, and then I go into the bathroom, flush the loo, turn on the shower, and run water in the basin — and then let my laughter gush out. I laugh until I cry and cry until I scream.

This is the Mad Hatter's tea party, and I am Alice. Oh, Dad! Daddy!

I take my time dressing, trying to think my way out of this mess. Somehow I have to get through to them.

As I go downstairs, I hear them talking in the kitchen.

Mother is laughing. "Oh, she'll be so pleased."

I walk into the kitchen, and they both look up from their tea and muffins, smiling.

"Here you are, Catherine," Grandma says, as if she had just arrived and was seeing me for the first time. "We were talking about your birthday present. You'll be sixteen in just one week. Aren't you excited?"

I search Mother's face for some sign that she remembers the brawl upstairs. Her make-up is perfect, and I can't guess what's underneath it.

"Sure, I guess I'm excited," I say. I take the orange juice from the refrigerator and pour myself a big glass. My hands are shaking. There is no way I can bring up the subject of my father again. They are playing the grown-up game of Let's-Pretend-the-World-Is-Wonderful.

"Wait until you see what your grandmother is giving you," Mother says, exchanging smiles with Grandma St John. "You're a lucky girl."

It's so easy for me to slip into the game. I'm happy to do it. I smile, even though I know I'm betraying my father. "Give me a hint, Grandma. You always give me a good hint."

She smiles a wrinkled smile. "You bad girl, you. Sometimes you guess if I give you too good a hint."

I'm having trouble blinking away tears. My heart is breaking for all of us. "Give me half a hint, then. The way you used to."

She remembers the old game from my childhood and laughs. "You're a scamp, Catherine. All right. You've talked me into it. Half of it is red. How's that?"

I pretend to think, then shake my head. "You wouldn't give me half a red wagon, would you, Grandma?"

She and Mother laugh and nod wisely to each other. "She's like you, Silvie. Beautiful and bright."

I bend down and hug her, inhaling her lilac cologne and loving her even though she is an impossible, terrible old woman.

When my father comes home from his walk, Grandma and Mother are gone and I am doing my laundry. He comes in the back door, passing the laundry room on his way somewhere. His jacket is wet, and I realize for the first time that it's raining.

"Did you have a good walk, Dad?" I call out.

He stops, turns, and stares at me. For a moment I am not certain that he remembers me.

"Well, now, Cat, I enjoy walking in the rain." His smile looks like a grimace because he is so pale and the dark circles under his eyes are purple-black. "The maple trees in the park are beginning to leaf. Did you know that?"

I nod. "Spring is here, thank goodness. Winter seemed awfully long."

"Winter, yes," he says sadly. He is wringing his

hands. "Yes, well, excuse me, Cat. I have work to do in my study."

He shambles off, and I realize that he is old. Not so much in years, I guess, but in some other way I can't name. He is caught in winter and can't get free.

He stays in his study all day. When I call him for lunch, he says he is not hungry, so I eat alone.

Charlie calls me in the afternoon. "Would you like to go for a ride tonight?" he asks. "We could stop for hamburgers somewhere. I need to talk to you."

I'll just bet you do, I think, grinning. "I can't, but thanks, Charlie. My family has plans."

We never have plans any more, but lately this has been a convenient excuse. Charlie argues, though.

"I won't keep you out very long."

"I really can't." I want to ask him how Suzy is, or if he's planning on suggesting that we go steady. No, stop that, Cat. Poor Charlie is in an awful bind.

He sighs. "Maybe tomorrow night?"

"I'm busy then, too." This is getting tiresome. Why don't I just tell him the truth? I don't think we're ever going to be more than acquaintances — we don't even have enough in common to be friends.

His mother and my mother would object. Mother would peck away and peck away until I'd end up calling Charlie back and apologizing, just to get some peace.

Eventually we'll drift apart, Charlie and I. Time will take care of it. Isn't that how adults handle things like this? Wait long enough and the problem no longer exists.

Charlie and I exchange some meaningless comments and I hang up. I give this stupid relationship just a little more time while I stall around and Charlie yearns for Suzy. Then he'll graduate from high school and out of my life.

Patience, Cat, I tell myself. You don't need another scene after this morning. Not for a long, long time.

Mother comes home in triumph, earlier than usual.

She holds up two fingers. "I finalized two sales today," she tells us. "We're rich, practically. Solvent, anyway. Why don't we go out to celebrate?"

It's been months since we did something like this. I look quickly at my father and see him smiling.

"Well, now, Silvie, I think you've got a good idea there. I'll call for reservations at Blanc's. Would you like that?"

He potters off happily to make his call.

"See?" Mother says. "He's just been tired and worried. You're too young to understand these things."

I want to believe, and so I do. I'm halfway up the stairs when Mother interrupts me. "Catherine?"

"What?" I ask quickly. Now what?

"I'm taking next Sunday off," she says. "I've already arranged it. Your grandmother has a special surprise for you, so we'll go in to Seattle to celebrate your birthday. You don't mind if it's a day late, do you?"

"No. That sounds great." I wonder if I should tell her that Cameron and I are planning a picnic on the

51

day before, my actual birthday. And Cameron said something about driving to Seattle for dinner and a movie.

"Is something wrong?" Mother asks.

I wake up and shake my head. "No. Everything's perfect." I'll talk to Dad and her about the picnic later.

The curtains in my room are open, and through the drizzle outside I see Cameron's light burning, but his room is empty. I stand at my window for a moment, thinking about our plans for a picnic at the farm.

The apple blossoms will be out by then, and if the day is warm we can sit under the trees, Cameron and I. And maybe my father. And everything will be all right.

"Catherine? Are you almost ready? Your father got us reservations in half an hour."

"In a minute," I call out to Mother.

Everything has to be all right.

My father drives us to the restaurant, paying careful attention to the traffic and the slippery roads. I sit in the back, my fingernails digging into my palms, but nothing goes wrong. He doesn't thump his fist on the wheel. He doesn't even hum to himself.

We order our favourite things and my parents sip white wine while we're waiting for the food. My mother is beautiful and my father is handsome — they smile at each other and I smile at them. The knotted muscles in my neck relax.

A few feet away, two waiters collide and one of them drops his tray. The dishes crash and clatter, and someone begins to laugh.

I hear my father groan, and I turn in my chair. He has covered his face with his trembling hands. His dark hair falls over his forehead, and I realize with horror that he is crying.

My mother reaches out to touch him. "Richard?" She glances around and I follow her glance. No one is looking at us yet.

"Richard, do you want to go home?" she asks in a low voice.

He does not hear her. He is listening to his own private nightmares, and she is not invited.

I stand up suddenly, surprising myself. "Let's go home."

People are looking at us now. And why not? My mother is leaning towards my father, speaking words to a deaf man, and I am standing across from them, trying to pretend that I don't know them. My father is weeping audibly.

Our waiter rushes at us, fluttering his hands in the air. "Is something wrong?" he asks Mother.

"My husband is ill. We have to leave now."

"It couldn't have been the wine," the waiter protests. "That was an excellent wine."

I feel the crazy laughter bubbling up again. "Come on," I say to Mother. "Take his arm and let's go."

She obeys me like a child. She takes my father's arm and steers him towards the door. People stare as we pass.

I hold my head up proudly as I lead the way, but when we are outside I collapse inside myself.

"Help me, Catherine," Mother says.

My father's legs are shaking and he can barely walk. I grab his arm and Mother and I drag him to the car.

"The keys. Where are the keys?" Mother asks Father.

He can't hear her. I reach into his pocket and pull out the keys.

"Quick, unlock the door before he falls," she says.

I open the car door and we shove my father into the back seat. We stand there, Mother and I, looking at each other.

"I'll drive," she says and takes the keys from me.

I ride home in the back, sitting behind my father, but I look out at the night and think about Cameron.

In a few moments we'll be home and then I'll go up to my room, open the curtains, and turn on the light. When Cameron sees me, I'll climb out of the window and fly over the fence.

We manage to pull Father from the car and get him in the front door. He is trembling and apologizing. His legs don't seem to work right, he says. He seems better now that we're home, and when I manage to escape them at last, he is sitting in his chair in front of the television.

Cameron's room is dark. In fact, his whole house is dark.

The rain falls all night long.

❂ SIX ❂

DEAR SHEILA
My father is really sick. Why doesn't
somebody do something?
I can't stand any more of this. If nobody else
cares, then neither do I.
Sincerely,

CAT ST JOHN

I call Mary Beth at nine-thirty.

"Are you going to church this morning?" I ask. I'm already dressed. My suit is new and feels strange, as if it belonged to someone else. I don't especially want to go, but I'm not going to be a prisoner of everyone else's games any more.

"You want to go with me?" Mary Beth squeals. "Really, I thought . . . I mean, I didn't know . . ."

Poor Mary Beth. If she didn't work so hard on being tactful, she'd be more tactful.

"I'd like a lift," I break in.

"Oh, sure," she says. "I'll be by your place in ten minutes. Is that okay?"

"It's exactly right," I tell her.

Mother is standing behind me when I hang up. She's ready to leave for the open house at the new development. Life goes on as usual, even though we had an end-of-the-world disaster last night. The kitchen has been sterilized and the living room rendered dust-free and totally unlivable, so everything must be all right. Right?

"Are you going to church?" she asks. "That's nice. You need to get out more."

I brush at invisible fluff on my dark blue skirt. "I haven't been to church since January," I say. That's a dig. I want to hurt her this morning. "I found out in January that God doesn't answer prayers, so there really hasn't been any point in going to church."

I look at her and see the ugly flush blooming under her make-up. She blinks — her green eyes blaze.

"Are you giving God a second chance?" she asks. "He'll be overwhelmed at your generosity."

I feel as though my breath has been knocked out of me. Who is this woman? My mother would never say something like that. Remarks like that are only made by people who won't play the games.

She turns away from me, but not before I see the lines on her face. I am shocked by them. When did they appear? Last night? In January?

The front door slams, and I hear her car start.

I'm not going to care about this.

My father isn't up yet, which is unusual, but I'm not going to care about that either. I check my lipstick in the hall mirror and congratulate myself on looking as good as I do, everything considered.

Mary Beth honks at the front for me and I hurry out, slamming the door behind me.

She is smiling when I slip into the car beside her. "You look nice," she tells me.

"So do you."

She drives up the block, glancing at me once. "I've missed going to church with you. Everyone asks about you."

I'm feeling embarrassed now. I don't need to be treated like the prodigal son, and I try to change the subject.

"I've been thinking about the dance," I say. "I still don't want to go — I really do have other plans — but I'll help with the decorations."

"Yea! Oh boy, am I relieved! With only three people doing the decorating, there wasn't much hope we could pull it off."

"Three people?" I ask. "What happened to everybody?"

She shrugs. "After you dropped out, the kids just sort of drifted away one by one."

"We need more than four decorators," I say. "I'll ask Cameron to help."

"Fat chance. Cameron never helps with anything like that."

"You're right. He calls it kid stuff."

"Why don't you ask Charlie?"

We're pulling into the church parking lot, and I figure that this is a good place to be honest. "I'd better not. We won't be going out any more, so . . ."

Mary Beth whistles under her breath. "How come?"

"My mother likes him. His mother likes him. Suzy likes him. I don't like him."

"Suzy! You know about Suzy and Charlie?"

She's parked the car, so I open the door and hop out. "I was the last to know and the last to care, too."

She locks up the car and follows me to the church door. "I'm glad you don't care," she whispers. "I think Charlie is the most incredible jerk."

We see some kids we know standing just inside the door and they smile at me. I'm feeling more and more awkward, as if I had been away for years instead of months.

We sit in the back, where the young people gather in a shined-up, perfumed, blow-dried flock, like exotic birds in a tree full of sparrows. The rest of the church fills with adults looking worried. Everyone knows that young people don't have worries, so I suppose they envy us. We are the ones who just graduated from the children's chapel a few years ago and have yet to enter the School of Hard Knocks. I celebrate the wonderfulness of being young and carefree.

Dear Sheila, I think, watch me fly away.

I find myself looking at my watch every ten minutes and staring out the window the rest of the time, wishing I hadn't come. Last night's rain has left trees and lawns sparkling in the Sunday morning sunshine, and the church flower beds blaze with daffodils and tulips. The farm will be so beautiful today that my heart thumps when I think of it.

In the middle of my sleepless night I had decided that I wouldn't go out there with my father any more, but I won't have my driving licence for nearly a week, so maybe I can make an exception. Maybe I can go this evening and nothing awful will happen. I'll use all my willpower. I'll bend life to meet my wishes.

And then I'll stop thinking about it.

After church Mary Beth drives us to the ice-cream store near the shopping mall and we order hot-fudge sundaes.

"Let it be my treat," she says. "I'm the one with a job, and I'm earning so much money I hardly know what to do with it."

"Do you like working?" I spread a paper napkin over my lap and dig into the ice-cream.

Mary Beth shrugs and licks her spoon. "I'd rather inherit a million dollars, but the job's not bad. Actually, it's fun most of the time."

"I could get a job," I say, thinking while I'm talking. "My folks wouldn't like it, but I'll be sixteen in a few days, and practically everybody works when they're sixteen."

"The Hamburger Palace is looking for someone to work the afternoon shift," Mary Beth says. "That's more fun than the late shift, but the tips aren't as good. Why don't you apply? I can put in a good word for you with the manager."

"Do you think he'd hire me?" I ask. The thought of a job makes me dizzy. All that money. And I'd be out of the house. And if I saved up enough money, lots of money, I could move away.

I could really move away.

"Sure," Mary Beth is saying. "And the manager is a woman. She's okay, I guess. Just don't let her scare you."

I'm hardly listening to her because I'm listening to me. Move away. Could I do that? Is it legal?

It's impossible, that's all.

No, it's not. In another year I'll be out of high school. If I had enough money of my own I could move to Seattle and go to college there. I could live in a dorm and only go home at weekends. Or never, if I wanted it that way. I could just telephone my parents once in a while, and I'd be very careful not to ask how they are. How my father is.

If I don't think too much about this idea it will sound possible, and I can soar on this high feeling until everything straightens out.

"Let's go to a movie," I say. "We'll go dutch. I've got my allowance."

I don't want this feeling to end. Right now, Mary Beth is the best friend I have, and I want the day to go on and on.

While we're driving to the cinema, Mary Beth says, "Can I ask you something?"

Whenever anyone says that, I know I won't like what's coming, but what else can I say except "Go ahead. Ask."

"When you quit the dance committee I thought maybe you were mad at me. But later, when I thought about it, I wondered if maybe you quit because of what happened with your dad. Was that it?"

The day turns cold even though the sky is bright. I should never have said the word January to my mother this morning because now I'll have to deal with January all day long. It's like a Gypsy curse — if you say the wrong word, you have to carry it around like a cross.

"I'd rather not talk about it," I say, slumping down in my seat.

Mary Beth apologizes, then adds, "But is your father better now?"

"Yes." I lie. "Mary Beth, aren't we going to be late for the movie?"

"No, we'll be right on time."

The afternoon has been spoiled.

After the movie Mary Beth reminds me again that I'm to help out decorating the gym on Thursday and Friday afternoons. "But we'll have to do most of the work Saturday morning."

I remember suddenly that I was going to take my driving test on Saturday morning and I tell her.

"You could take the test afterwards," she says. "We should be done by noon."

"Sure," I say, but my mind is whirling. By noon Cameron and I should be at the farm. And if I have my licence, I can drive us. We won't need to ask my father. We can spend the day there alone and then drive to Seattle.

"How long did it take you to get your licence?"

"Gee," she says slowly, "I don't really remember. I had to wait forever, and the driving test seems like it takes forever, too, but I guess it's only about fifteen minutes. You'd better plan on a couple of hours, though, because the place will be jammed on a Saturday."

A couple of hours. Now I wish I hadn't told Mary Beth that I would help her.

It'll work out, I think. I'll just concentrate and it will all work out.

When she stops at my house, I see my father digging in the flower bed under the living room window.

"Hi, Mr St John!" Mary Beth yells.

My father stands up and turns around. When he sees Mary Beth, he starts towards us, smiling. "Why, now, it's little Suzy. I believe you've grown more beautiful since the last time I saw you."

"This is Mary Beth, Dad." I'm ready to cry.

"Of course!" Dad is wringing his hands again. "Wonderful to see you."

Mary Beth smiles, but her eyes flicker from me to my father uncertainly.

"Thank you," she says cautiously, and she waves good-bye.

"Now there goes a nice girl," my father says. "I like to see you having a good time with your friends."

"Sure." I run up the steps to the front door. My mother's car is in the drive.

She meets me inside the door. "Where have you been?"

"Mary Beth and I went to a movie after church," I say, trying to slip past her and get to the stairs.

"You should have called me."

"You weren't home," I respond angrily.

"You should have called your father." She is wearing an apron over her suit skirt, and I smell chicken frying. It's later than I thought.

"He wasn't worried."

She can't argue with that. He probably didn't know I was gone until he saw me coming home.

She lets me go up to my room without any more discussion. I know I should have called. Now I feel guilty because I had a good time.

Well, I almost had a good time. January kept interfering.

In January my parents were chaperones at the winter dance. My father was just beginning to get a little strange then. Or, as my mother would say, he was just beginning to show signs of fatigue.

In other words, when it came time to leave for the dance, my father wasn't home. He had been gone all day, and we hadn't heard a word from him.

I had a date with Charlie, naturally, and he was waiting on the porch. Mother was on the phone, calling everyone she could think of to see if Dad was there.

"I'll leave in a couple of minutes," she called after me. "I'm sure he'll remember and be there before nine."

He wasn't. Mother came just as the band began

playing, apologizing to other chaperones, making excuses for my father. And then I forgot all about Dad, because in spite of Charlie's being an incredible jerk, he is a good dancer.

In those ancient times I used to have a lot of friends and I loved the dances.

My father showed up at ten. He stood in the doorway of the gym watching the dancers, nodding gravely at the kids he knew as they passed him.

He was wearing his dinner jacket and black tie. But the other chaperones were wearing sport clothes. And the kids were wearing jeans. Some of them began to laugh.

My father laughed, too, as he walked up to Mother, Charlie and me. But he didn't know what was funny.

"Richard, what on earth is the matter with you?" my mother whispered furiously. "I told you this was very informal."

You could see the light dawning for my father as he looked around him. Beads of perspiration shone on his face.

"Oh, I'm so sorry," he apologized. He turned this way and that, gesturing, as if everyone were watching and listening. And everyone was.

"I don't know what I was thinking of," he said.

Mary Beth's father joined us, grinning. "Well, well, Richard, where have you been?"

We waited for my father to say something witty and make us all laugh with relief. Instead he said,

"Well, now, I guess I must have had a lot of errands."

The silence was awful. Mary Beth skidded up then and danced around my father like a two-year-old.

"You look wonderful!" she cried. "Why don't we all dress up for the next dance?"

The silence rolled over her and she stopped talking, looking around bewilderedly.

My father's eyes filled with tears. "I'm sorry," he mumbled.

"But what's wrong?" Mary Beth chirped.

"Be quiet, Mary Beth," I said. I looked at Mother for rescue.

"Come over here and have a glass of punch, Richard," she said, and she pulled his sleeve.

"I'm sorry," my father repeated, and he stumbled towards the door.

"Jeez," Charlie groaned. "Will somebody please tell me what's going on?"

"Richard couldn't stay," my mother said brightly. "He has another engagement."

And so the games began.

I change clothes and hang up my suit. As I pass my window I can see Cameron's parents working in their garden. He mows the grass and she clips the edges.

As I watch, Cameron comes out of the back door. He hands each of his parents a can of drink and together they sit on the bench under the pear tree. Cameron looks up, sees me watching, and raises one hand in greeting. I wave back.

We could go to the farm this evening and I'll tell him about next Saturday. We'll make plans.

And tomorrow after school I'll apply for a job.

I'm going to make everything all right.

❈ SEVEN ❈

I look up from the road and catch my breath. It seems to me that I can see a million million miles over the treetops, past this world and past all the others I've ever heard about, and on to unnamed stars. The sky is like a sapphire.

Reluctantly I look back at the road and concentrate on my driving. My father, sitting next to me, is turned in his seat, talking to Cameron.

Before we left I told him that I need driving practice. "I take my test on Saturday. Will you let me drive tonight?"

When he agreed, I let my sweaty fingers relax. He seemed all right this evening — he could have driven us out to the farm. But I don't want to take any chances.

My mother scowled, overhearing this conversation, but she was in a hurry, so she gathered up her briefcase and purse, kissed us both good-bye, and left for her office.

"Paperwork," she sighed. I didn't believe the sigh — I believed the relief I saw on her face as the door shut.

We are approaching the bridge and I cross my fingers, strong magic against the dark born in that cave in the gorge. The dark has always seemed more real to me than the fairies and shooting stars and talking caterpillars. I would rather believe in the fairies, but I don't have a choice. I know the dark.

We zip over the bridge and rush through the clear evening towards the farm. I uncross my fingers.

The trip seems to take longer tonight, or maybe I'm just nervous driving. I'm relieved when I turn into the drive and stop the car in front of the house.

"Why, I believe the grass has grown three inches since I was here last," my father says when he gets out of the car. What's left of the old lawn is shaggy and coarse, and weeds sprout everywhere. I see a dandelion blooming near the fence, and I walk over to pick it.

Cameron follows me and takes the dandelion, holding it under my chin.

"You like butter," he says. "And I like you."

"You're supposed to do that with buttercups." I push his hand away. Is my father watching?

No, he is walking towards the old barn, fishing

through his pockets as he goes. He pulls out keys and opens the padlock on the door.

"I'm going to get out the mower," he shouts back at us. "You kids run along."

We walk around the house and sit on the porch, just where we always sit. The apple blossoms are out. In the evening light they look like fairy bride bouquets. I inhale, intoxicating myself with the scent.

"Somebody must have farmed this place," Cameron says. "Who had it before your grandfather?"

I hug my knees. "His father. He was the real farmer."

Cameron sighs and he sounds contented. "Living here would be great."

I hold my breath. "Yes," I whisper finally.

The swallows glide and soar over the trees. I can hear the frogs at the pond croaking.

With a roar, the petrol mower starts up, and we burst out laughing.

"Let's walk down to the pond where it's quiet," Cameron says. "I have to talk to you."

I'm afraid. I walk beside him through the wild orchard grass, blind to everything.

"Tell me now," I say. "You're scaring me."

He crunches my hand in his big one. "I'm scaring me, too," he tells me. "I've been thinking about something ever since I was accepted in college. I don't want to go. So last night my folks and I went over to Dinsmore's and we talked to him for a while."

So that's where they were. With Cameron's music

teacher. I was afraid to ask him why he wasn't home last night — afraid he was with Suzy. Or someone else.

We're at the pond and Cameron shifts restlessly from one foot to the other.

I shake his arm. "So tell me what's going on."

"Boy, I hope I'm not making a big mistake," he mutters.

I shake his arm again. "Wake up and talk to me!"

He pulls me down on the log beside the pond and puts his arm around my shoulders. "I'm going to audition at the music school in Seattle this week."

I am stupefied. I think of Cameron at the last school concert, when he played Chopin and shrugged off the applause. Music is just his hobby. He is some sort of mathematical genius like his parents, and he is supposed to be going to his father's old college in the fall. Three thousand miles away.

I stare at him. "Are you kidding me? This sounds like another one of your big jokes."

"It's no joke, Cat. If you laugh, I'll shove you into the pond." His voice cracks, and I know he's not kidding.

"How long have you been thinking about this? Why didn't you tell me before?"

"I couldn't make up my mind." He picks up a small pebble and throws it into the water. The frogs stop croaking and a duck hiding in the reeds mutters crossly at us.

"And now you're sure?"

He nods, then laughs. "I hope I'm sure. I think so."

"Wow." I try to think of Cameron as a professional musician and I can't. "What do your folks say about this?"

He shrugs. "They told me to try music school for a while, and if I change my mind, that's okay. They hope I'll change my mind, though. There's never been a musician in the family. They're embarrassed."

Far away the mower sputters and roars. The sky is slowly darkening in the east, but in the west it explodes with gold streaks. The clouds there bloom pink and purple. I am afraid to be happy.

He'll be near me, not three thousand miles away.

We lean together, not talking. The pond glistens like a dark mirror in the fading light, smooth and placid. The mower stops, and we both turn and look back towards the house.

"Look!" I whisper.

In the still evening, the cherry blossoms are dropping, falling straight to the orchard grass. Silent and white they fall, first only a few, and then the orchard is misted with them.

"I thought the wind always blew them down, but there is no wind," Cameron whispers.

I cannot speak for the wonder of it. There is not a sound anywhere, and the petals fall, starring the grass.

"Let's walk through them," Cameron says.

We get up slowly and move towards the trees. We are almost there when a light wind suddenly stirs the branches. The petals swirl madly, dancing over us.

Cameron grabs both my hands and swings me around in circles.

"It's time to dance."

"Wait," I say, bending to tug my shoes and socks off. He pulls his off, too, throwing them out into the dark after mine. The grass is wet and cold around my ankles — my feet tingle as we run to the centre of the orchard.

The moon is full. I see it when I tip my head back as Cameron swings me around. Our feet hiss in the grass. We spin faster. My arms are being pulled from their sockets.

The cherry trees are a ghostly blur around us. Petals cling to Cameron's dark hair. I feel them on my face, and I drop my head back again to look up at the moon.

The world is silver and white and a deep, aching blue. Cameron stops suddenly and catches me in his arms.

"Oh, Cat, I'm glad we came."

Before I can answer, he bends his head, grins suddenly, and then kisses me.

My arms lock behind his neck and I close my eyes. His lips are cool at first, but then grow warm as he pulls me closer.

He begins to turn me around again, at first slowly and then faster, and then he pulls his face away, ending the kiss. We are spinning and laughing while the wind shakes white magic down on us in the old orchard planted before our fathers were born.

We slow and stop, gasping and laughing, and then I see an angry red eye gleaming under a tree. My heart has stopped.

My father's cigarette glows as he inhales, and I am almost sick with panic. Did he see us? Was he watching when Cameron kissed me?

We let each other go, and Cameron steps away from me.

My father moves out from under the tree. "Why, now," he says mildly, "I do believe the two of you must be the last of the April dancers."

What is he talking about? I move towards Cameron. He takes my hand. "I think you're right, Mr St John. We are the last."

"Once, a long time ago," my father begins, then he stops for a moment and clears his throat. "I'm a little tired. I'll wait in the car for the two of you."

He walks away rapidly and disappears into the dark.

I'm getting cold. "What was he talking about? What did he mean when he said we are the last of the April dancers?"

Cameron is looking into the dark. "I don't know," he says sadly.

"But you said we were the last of them."

"We are," he says and kisses my forehead. "Don't worry about it. Come on, let's find our shoes, Cinderella. The ball is over for tonight."

I can find only one of my shoes, and after half an hour of searching we give up.

Our moon shadows move ahead of us as we walk around the house. The building looks new, silvered with moonlight instead of the tired old yellow paint it wore when we came.

My father is sitting in the back seat of the car, smoking, waiting. Cameron gets in front with me.

"Did you get the lawn all mowed?" he asks my father.

"Why, I believe I did," my father says. He rolls down a window to let out his smoke, and I start the car.

The trip back doesn't take as long as the trip there, because I don't want to go home. Even though I cross my fingers going over the bridge, the dark is following me.

I know that this evening and the dance in the orchard are over and finished. Will I remember them when I am as old as my father? Will Cameron remember?

When I stop the car in front of Cameron's house, he reaches for my hand and squeezes it for a quick moment.

"See you, Cat. Good night, Mr St John."

He shuts the door and taps twice on the top of the car. I wave and turn the car out into the street, my bare toes cold on the accelerator.

"Beautiful night," my father says. He clears his throat and coughs. "It's a little chilly, though."

"You sound like you're coming down with a cold," I say, making small talk while I drive around the block to our house.

"Yes." He coughs again. "That Cameron. You like him, don't you?"

I pull into our drive. "He's nice," I say, my mouth dry. Where is this conversation going?

Dad gets out of the back seat. "He's old for his age," he says. "You don't want to lose track of him, Cat. No matter what happens."

"I won't, Dad." Suddenly it's safe to smile.

My mother is watching television when we come in. She gets up and brings my father a cup of coffee. When I go upstairs, they are sitting together on the couch, silent and intent on the screen.

A moment after I turn on my light, my phone rings. I look across the back yards and see Cameron standing in his window, holding his phone.

"I wanted to talk to you once more," he says.

"Did you have a good time tonight?" I ask him.

"I wish we could have stayed there forever."

"So do I. Good night, Cameron."

"Good night, April dancer."

◼ EIGHT ◼

"How much longer are you going to take?"

I look up guiltily. The manager of the fast-food restaurant where Mary Beth works is standing over me. Her hands are on her hips, her skirt is wrinkled, and she looks hot and miserable. Maybe that's why she's so nasty.

"I was just looking over my application to see if I filled it out right." I hand her the sheet of paper, and she waits a moment too long before she takes it, letting me know she doesn't want it. Or me.

Frowning, she glances over the application. "You haven't worked before?" she asks, staring at me.

"Well, no," I admit. "But I get good grades at school."

She keeps staring, and I wish I had worn a different skirt. Maybe my shoes are wrong. I fidget. My fingers pluck at the ends of my hair.

"That hair. You'll have to do something with it. Cut it, I guess. We can't have hair hanging in everybody's food."

I clench my hands together in my lap. "I'll braid it, they way Mary Beth does."

"Who?"

I see Mary Beth halfway across the dining area watching us as she wipes off a table. "Mary Beth," I say again, louder. "The girl right over there."

The manager looks over her shoulder and then back at me. "I'm really too busy to spend any more time with you. We'll call you if we need you."

I say "Thank you" to her back as she walks away and bite my lips to keep the tears out of my eyes.

She's a horrible, ugly bitch and I hate her forever. All I did was ask for a job, but she treated me as if I were going to rob the place.

Mary Beth rushes towards me, smiling nervously. "How'd it go?" she asks under her breath.

Before I can answer, the manager shouts Mary Beth's name.

"See you later," I say and I head for the door.

When I'm outside I draw my first full breath for the last half hour. My face burns with anger. How do kids get jobs? Do they go from place to place collecting rejections and insults until someone who is desperate for help finally hires them? Mary Beth made it sound so easy.

I head for home, walking the ten blocks hugging my books to my chest and telling myself that this didn't matter. I can apply somewhere else tomorrow. There's sure to be a job for me in Waterford. I'll keep trying until I find it.

At home I find a package on the porch and a jumble of mail in the box. My father's car is in the drive so he's probably home, but apparently he didn't hear the postman. I juggle books, mail, and the package while I open the door and see that the package is addressed to me.

It will be a birthday gift from my aunt Leah in California. She was my uncle James's wife, and after he died she moved away. I haven't seen her since, but she never forgets me at Christmas and on my birthday. She sends glamorous gifts, things my parents never think of buying. Once she sent me ten different necklaces — all in one box. Another time she sent a jade bracelet.

I let everything slip from my arms to the couch.

"Dad?"

He doesn't answer, so I walk out to the kitchen, looking for him. Through the window I see him working in his little garden. I knock on the glass, and he looks up and waves.

I go back to the living room and tear the brown wrapping paper from the package. Inside, the box is wrapped in bright flowered paper with a card taped to it. My birthday is five days away, but it's okay to read a card ahead of time, so I sit down and open the envelope.

When you get this, I'll be in Hong Kong.
Sixteenth birthdays are special — so have the
best time you've ever had. I'll be thinking about
you on Saturday, kiddo. And next time you
write, tell me about the farm.
    Love,
    LEAH

I squeeze the big box. It's soft and light, and I'm tempted to open it right now. But instead I'll take it with me on Saturday and open it at the farm. Aunt Leah loved the farm, and she'd like that.

"Why, that must be from Leah." Dad stands in the doorway, grinning.

"Yes, it is." I'd like to tell him about the horrible time I had with the manager of the restaurant, but he doesn't know I'm looking for a job and I'm not sure how he'll take the news. I sort through the mail and hand him a long white envelope.

"This is for you. The rest is junk mail."

He smiles again when he reads the return address on the envelope. I see that his hands are shaking a little.

"Well now, I think this might be about that interview I had way back in February," he says.

I am suddenly filled with hope and excitement. "For a job, you mean? Do you have a job?"

He laughs shakily and coughs. "Why, could be, Cat. Could be. I'll just have a look."

He heads for his study, as if he couldn't bear to have me watch when he gets his good news.

I wonder if that's how I'll feel when I finally get a job. Won't I want to share the excitement, either? Will I go to my room and gloat all by myself?

I wait but my father doesn't come out of his study. I want to run and knock on the door, but instead I sort through the junk mail again and pretend to myself that I'm interested in it.

If my father goes back to work, maybe he'll be all right again. Everything could be the way it used to be.

I wait and hear my father coughing in the study. I can't stand it any more. I go to the study door and knock.

"Dad? Did you get the job?"

He coughs, and I hear his chair scrape on the floor.

"Dad? Can I come in?"

He coughs again. "I'm pretty busy in here, Cat. Is it important?"

He didn't get the job. I am humiliated for him, knowing that he must feel the way I do. I take my birthday present upstairs to my room and drop it on my bed.

My phone rings. It's Cameron, and he sounds strange.

"Where have you been? I've been waiting for you to come home."

"I went over to the shopping mall," I tell him evasively. "What's up?"

"Listen, your dad came over right after I got home from school."

"To your house?" I ask, surprised.

"Of course to my house. And listen, Cat, he gave me something." Cameron sounds upset, and my imagination is doing cartwheels.

"What did he give you?"

"This old watch. Look out the window."

I look and see Cameron dangling a round silver object near the window. It's too far away to be sure, but I'm sure anyway.

"That's Grandpa's watch."

I see Cameron shaking his head. "No, it actually belonged to your grandfather's father. The real farmer. Cat, it must be valuable, but he wouldn't take it back."

I can't think what to say for a moment.

"Cat, are you listening?"

"Of course I'm listening. I'm trying to think. I don't understand what's going on. Has he ever shown you the watch before?"

"No! I'd never even heard of it before. He just showed up at the front door and handed it to me. And Cat, listen. I think we'd better really talk about him now. I mean really talk."

My ears are ringing. I don't want to talk to anyone outside the family about my father, especially Cameron. If he knows how bad things are, he might wish he'd never met us. "He must want you to have the watch," I say, "so keep it."

"Cat, he's sick. And I don't just mean that lousy cold he's got. I worry about him — and you."

"He's just tired." I can't believe that I'm saying the same thing my mother says.

81

Cameron is silent, and my heart thumps while I wait for him to speak again.

"Maybe he should see a doctor or something," he says finally.

"My family is handling it." I lie, but I wish I dared tell him he's right. I change the subject. "Do you know yet which day you audition? Tell me about that."

I hear Cameron sigh. "Okay. I audition tomorrow afternoon."

"Are you going to practise a lot before then?" I'm struggling to keep the conversation on safe ground.

I guess Cameron can tell. "Sure I'll be practising. Why don't I call you back later tonight? And take it easy, okay?"

After we said good-bye, I close my curtains and change clothes, hanging up my skirt very carefully. Then I rearrange the things on my dressing table and straighten the books in my bookcase. If I keep this up I'll be so good at fussing that I can even wash the bars of soap in the bathroom — if Mother doesn't beat me to it.

Sometimes I almost understand her.

My mother comes home late and goes straight to the kitchen. She looks tired and angry.

"I'll help you with dinner," I offer, following her into the kitchen.

"Catherine, you know it drives me crazy to have anyone else in here when I'm cooking." She doesn't look at me.

"Then I'll set the table."

"I'd rather do it myself, thank you. At least here in my own kitchen everything goes the way it's supposed to go."

"Did you have an awful day?"

She is stripping plastic wrap off meat. "You might say that. One sale fell through at the last minute. I spent two hours waiting for people who never showed up and didn't even call to say they weren't coming."

We both hear Dad coughing in the other room. She glances quickly at me. "His cold sounds worse."

"I think it is," I say. "Maybe he should see a doctor."

Mother pauses for a moment, holding a steak over the counter. "You're right, but he hates to go. I'll talk to him about it."

The lines on her forehead seem to fade a little. Her mouth turns up at the corners. She is relieved, now that something besides dinner might turn out right.

The phone rings and I leave to answer it, for my father will let it go on ringing.

It's Mary Beth.

"You hated her, didn't you?" she says, and I don't have to ask whom she means. The manager.

"Well, I'm sure not going to vote her Miss Congeniality. How can you stand her?"

Mary Beth giggles. "I live from week to week on the hope that her boss will fire her. She makes lots of mistakes and we sure don't try to keep him from finding out."

I have to laugh. "Good luck. In the meantime I

don't think you'll be seeing me at work there. She wouldn't give me a job taking out the rubbish."

"Don't let it get to you," Mary Beth says quickly. "I tried for a dozen jobs before I got this one. Just apply everywhere and keep smiling."

"Sure, keep smiling."

"And now for some good news. There'll be six of us working on the decorations Thursday and Friday and eight on Saturday morning. That's enough to do a good job so there's no chance we'll run late Saturday. You'll be done in time to get to the State Patrol office by noon."

We agree to have lunch together tomorrow and check out our decorating supplies, and then I go back to the kitchen. Dinner is ready, and my mother lets me carry the salad to the table. She is smiling. The kitchen is immaculate.

Halfway through dinner my father begins to cough again, but when Mother offers to call the doctor, he says he'll do it tomorrow. He leaves the table and we hear him in the living room, choking and gasping.

He hasn't said a word about the letter he got today. I don't say anything about it, either, but I tell Mother about the package from Aunt Leah.

"And she's in Hong Kong," she says wistfully. "She must travel six months out of every year."

"She's rich, I'll bet," I say. I finish the last of my salad and look at Mother, waiting for a response.

She tastes her tea and then says, "James left her well-off."

"Why doesn't she ever come here for a visit?" Aunt Leah travels everywhere but here, and we never go to see her. Not even Grandma St John ever sees her.

Mother frowns and shrugs. "She never could get along with your grandmother."

"That I can believe," I say.

Mother looks up at me. "Catherine," she says warningly.

"But Grandma's impossible," I say. "She's never been nice to Daddy, not ever. She talks about Uncle James as if he died yesterday."

"Catherine." Mother warns me again.

Stubbornly I go on. "I don't blame Aunt Leah. I wouldn't visit her, either."

Mother stands up and begins to clear the table. "You don't know what you're talking about. Leah and James would probably have ended up getting a divorce if he had lived. Grandma didn't think she was right for James. It wasn't working out."

"Why not?" I persist.

Exasperated, she puts the plates back down on the table with a thump. "If you must know, Leah is too independent. She's actually rather eccentric. James had business ambitions and a busy schedule, but Leah wanted to live just the way she does now. And she's doing it on James's money. Grandma gets upset every time she thinks about it."

After Mother leaves the room, I wander into the living room. My father is sitting in a chair in the darkest corner, and his hand taps against the cushion.

He is hearing his own music again and he doesn't even see me.

"Dad?"

He looks up, surprised. "Who's there?"

"It's me, Dad. Cat."

He grins, and I see how thin his face is now. "It's dark in here, and you look like your mother tonight. Is that a new hair style?"

"No, Dad." My mother wears her hair short and sleek, while mine is pulled back from my face and hangs halfway down my back. He is breaking my heart.

"Dad," I say softly, "why did you give Grandpa's watch to Cameron?"

"Why, because I wanted him to have it after I saw the two of you in the orchard. Are we going out to the farm tonight? It's a beautiful evening."

"I have too much homework. And you have a bad cold. We'll go later in the week, okay?"

"Why, that will be just fine. I'm sorry we can't make it tonight. Sorry about this cough, too. Things will be better very soon, I promise you. Everything will be much better."

"I know," I tell him.

DEAR SHEILA
Did you dance with my father in the orchard?
Sincerely,

CAT ST JOHN

❈ NINE ❈

I fill out another application, this time at a coffee shop, and the manager smiles at me. But she tells me she probably won't hire me. She is chubby and red-faced, and her pale blue eyes shine. "I like you and I'd hire you if we weren't always in such a rush here. I just won't have time to train you. Sorry."

I wander through the mall, looking in shop windows, stalling for time. Cameron is in Seattle now, auditioning for the music school, and if I go home too soon I'll have to sit and wait for him to get back and tell me his news.

For practice, I ask for an application at the toy shop and fill it in at the counter. The clerk tells me crisply that someone will contact me. I can tell they won't.

I leave, too disappointed to pretend that I don't care.

I'm getting to be an expert at filling in job applications. Cheer up, I tell myself. Sooner or later someone will hire me and I can start saving money. My own money. And next year I'll surprise my parents.

"I can take care of myself now," I'll say. "I'm old enough and I have enough money."

That's as far as I dare think. What comes after the big announcement is hard to imagine, and it worries me. Will I find an apartment in Seattle? Move into a dormitory at the university? Will Cameron be there or in the East? Will he get into music school?

My feet hurt and I'm tired. I decide to wait at home.

I hear my father coughing when I open the front door.

"I thought you were going to the doctor today."

He is sitting in the living room, wearing his gardening clothes, and his old shoes are muddy. He blinks at me.

"Why, I guess I was. I must have forgotten."

I look at my watch, exasperated with him. Can't he take care of himself? Can't he remember anything?

"It's nearly four. Why don't you call and see if you can get an appointment now? I'll drive you."

He stands up and I see he is embarrassed. "Why, that's right. You're going to be taking your driving test in a few days. You need practice."

"Yes, Daddy. Now you call the doctor's office and change clothes. I'm going upstairs for a few minutes."

I have to walk away quickly because he is scaring me. Doesn't he know he's sick? His cough is worse than ever.

I hear him on the phone when I walk upstairs. His voice is hesitant, as if he were ashamed of having a bad cold. I can't bear to listen.

I look out my bedroom window. Cameron's house has that dead look houses have when no one is home. I change clothes and go back downstairs, expecting that my father will have forgotten to change clothes or forgotten why he called the doctor's office.

He's already waiting for me, wearing clean clothes and shoes. "I have an appointment in fifteen minutes, Cat," he says. "Are you sure you want to drive in the afternoon traffic?"

I take the car keys from the tray on the table in the front hall. "I might as well get used to it," I tell him.

He is coughing constantly while I drive. I find a parking place in the lot next to the clinic and walk inside with him.

"I'll wait here for you," I tell him.

The nurse calls him in almost immediately, and I hear him coughing as he goes down the long hall to the examining rooms. It sounds as though he is coughing in a cave. I pick up a magazine and stare blindly at the glossy pages. Maybe the doctor will notice that my father has more wrong with him than just a cold. Aren't they trained to watch out for odd behaviour? Maybe Dad will call him Sheila. That will wake the doctor up quickly enough.

I'm grinning at the magazine, trying not to cry, when the nurse calls my name. Surprised, I look up. She stands in front of me wearing a white uniform and a patient look. Maybe she called me more than once. Maybe what my father has is catching or runs in families.

"The doctor would like to see you for a moment, while the technician is taking X-rays of your father."

I don't want to go with her, but I stand up and follow her. My face is burning. What did my father do? Maybe he did call the doctor Sheila. Or tried to give him his wrist watch. Or maybe he just started crying.

The doctor is standing behind his desk when I walk in, looking at the papers in a folder.

"How are you, Catherine?"

"Fine." I feel awkward and nervous. He sits. I sit.

"Your father probably has bronchitis," he says. "I've been trying to reach your mother, but she's not in her office. Do you know where she is?"

"Showing a house, I guess. But why do you want her?"

He glances at the folder again. "Oh, nothing urgent."

I don't believe him. "Is my father very sick?"

"I told you, it's probably bronchitis. He'll feel better in a few days. You can wait outside now, Catherine," he says.

I stand up, uncertain. "Do you want me to ask Mother to call you?"

"I'll try her office again later," he says, and he slips

out of the door next to his desk. The nurse materializes behind me.

"This way, Catherine," she murmurs.

I'm in and out of the office in a minute and a half, and I don't know any more than I did before except that my father probably has bronchitis.

I pick up the magazine again and look at a picture of a girl my age in a red-and-blue striped swimsuit. She is smiling. I can't smile.

Waiting in doctors' offices can seem long or short, depending on the reason I wait. If I'm going in for a booster shot, the wait is never long enough. If I'm waiting for someone else, I feel as if I'm growing old sitting there. When my father finally comes out, I am the only one left in the orange plastic room, and I have looked at all the magazines on the table.

My father is smiling and holding two prescriptions. "It's only a bad cold," he says. "He's given me a prescription for antibiotics, so I'll be fine again soon."

We walk together out of the door. "What's the other prescription for?" He has slipped both of them in his pocket, and he pats the pocket nervously when I look at him.

"Just a little something to help me get over this cough." I can tell he's lying.

I take him to the pharmacy nearest our house and wait while he goes in. When he comes out he is carrying a little bag.

"All set now?" I ask.

"Why, I think so."

Halfway home I have to slam on the brakes because the car ahead of me stops suddenly. My father slides down in his seat, white and shaking.

"I'm sorry, Dad. I couldn't hit that car."

"I know." His voice is faint and trembling. "Why, I know that, Cat. You're a fine driver. You'll pass that test without any trouble at all. When are you taking it?"

I turn right off the main road and head for our house. "Saturday at noon. I have to do something at school first, so I thought maybe you could pick me up there and we could go straight to the State Patrol office."

"Why, sure. And then we can go and celebrate."

I tell him about my plans as I park in our drive. "Cameron and I are going out to the farm for a picnic afterwards," I say, staring straight ahead. "You can come along if you like. He's asked me to go to dinner in Seattle that evening and then maybe see a movie. You can go, too, if you want."

Did I say it right? I don't want to hurt him, but I don't want him to go, either. I feel guilty again.

"But it's your birthday, Cat," he says as we get out of the car.

"I know, but Mom said Grandma wanted to do something special the next day at her place. So we'll celebrate both my birthday and my driving licence then, okay?"

I see him wringing his hands, and I hate myself so hard that I ought to shrivel up and die.

"I remember now," he says as he holds the front door open for me. "Your mother told me about that special plan of your grandmother's. Yes. That's what we'll do. We'll celebrate your birthday and your new licence on Sunday. And you and Cameron can go off on your picnic on Saturday. Right after we get back from the State Patrol office."

I shift my feet and stick my hands in the pockets of my jeans. "Everything will work out," I tell him. "I've got to start working on my history paper now."

When I'm upstairs my heart stops pounding. I pull out my history book but I can't concentrate. The afternoon sun is shining on my father's crazy garden and reflecting off the windows in Cameron's house. I'm sure he's not back yet. Is he nervous? He seemed that way in school today, but I didn't have much chance to talk to him.

I only caught quick glimpses of Charlie, too. He's avoiding me, I think, and I grin. So is Suzy. Every time she sees me, she blushes. How awful for them — to be happy and miserable at the same time. They think I don't know and are afraid that I do.

And they have to cope with Charlie's mother. Suzy isn't what she has in mind for her son. I wonder how she'd feel if she knew that my family isn't much better off than Suzy's now.

My mother is home — I hear her talking to my father, climbing the stairs quickly, and coming towards my door.

She knocks and opens the door. "Your father told

me you drove him to the doctor this afternoon. That was nice of you, Catherine."

"I need practice driving," I tell her. "There are only a few more days before I take the test."

"Oh, you'll pass. I'm sure of it." She closes the door, and I hear her humming as she goes to her own room.

The phone rings, startling me.

"Cat," Cameron says. "I'm back."

"How did it go?"

"I won't find out until Friday. I blew a couple of things on the piano, but I did okay on the flute."

"I didn't know you still played the flute."

"You have to have two instruments. I've got three, but they don't count guitar." He sighs. "Friday is three days away."

"Don't worry. You'll get in." I want to tell him I'm looking for a job so I can save money and live in Seattle next year, independent from my parents. But I'll wait until I'm sure I can do it.

"Are you going out to the farm tonight?" he asks.

"My dad's cold is worse. I drove him to the doctor today after school."

Cameron is silent for a long moment. "What did the doctor say?"

My stomach turns over. "He said Dad has a cold," I say sharply. "Don't start in on it again, Cameron."

"Okay, okay. Sorry. But —"

"No 'buts'," I say.

"Right. No 'buts'. Listen, Cat. I'd better hit the books."

I look out the window. He's wearing a shirt and tie.

"You look nice, Cameron."

He laughs his nice laugh and is quiet again. I hear his quick breaths.

"Cat," he says softly, "are we going to dance again on Saturday?"

"We're going to dance," I tell him. I'm light-headed, remembering the other night.

"See you, Cat."

I hang up, smiling, and watch him leave his room.

DEAR SHEILA
   Did you get my father's letter yet?
   If you think you and he are the last of the
April dancers, you're wrong. Cameron and I
dance in the orchard now.
   Sincerely,

   CAT ST. JOHN

▨ TEN ▨

A slow, gentle rain has fallen for most of the last two days. My father's cold is worse — or he's forgetting to take his antibiotics. I've asked him each day if he's taking his pills.

"Why, I believe so," he tells me every time.

He stays in bed all day, coughing. At dinner-time he joins us in the dining room, dressed, with his hair combed. His clothes hang on him. When he finishes eating he goes back upstairs. Mother scours the kitchen and everything else in sight and then goes back to her office.

We play the silent game. We rarely speak to each other, so I stay in my room when I'm not at school.

Now I sit in the cafeteria waiting for Cameron. He

is calling home for the second time today to find out if his mother has heard yet about his audition.

Suzy sits down next to me. Her face burns scarlet.

"Cat, I have to talk to you."

"Sure." I'm saving my sandwich until Cameron gets here. "Aren't you eating?"

She shakes her head. "I don't have an appetite."

"So what do you want to talk about?"

"Charlie."

"Stop worrying. I already know about you and Charlie. It's all right with me. Now, is everything okay or do you need a hug?"

She starts laughing. "I need a hug."

We throw our arms around each other, laughing.

"Now I can eat," she says and heads for the food counters. Charlie, the big coward, is waiting for her. I wave and he waves back. Thank goodness that's over. But where's Cameron?

Mary Beth is the next one to take the seat beside me.

"How did things go yesterday afternoon?" she asks.

"Well, stranger, what happened to you? We started moving the tables into the gym, then gave up and left. Are you going to be there today when we set them up?"

"Of course. Yesterday I wanted to pick up my pay cheque right after school and then come back, but when I walked in, the manager told me that the girl who was supposed to work that shift yesterday didn't show up, so I had to work it. She wouldn't even let me take time off to call you guys and let you know. Sometimes I hate working, even on payday."

"Don't knock it. So far I've put in six applications and no one wants me."

She takes a monstrous bite out of her hamburger. "Don't get discouraged," she says when she's had a chance to swallow. "You'll get a job."

I see Cameron standing at the door, looking around for me. "Mary Beth, would you mind awfully much if Cameron sits here? I was sort of saving this seat for him. He wants to tell me something."

"I'll bet there are a lot of things he'd like to tell you." She is laughing.

"What do you mean?" My face stings. I hate all the blushing that goes with being blonde.

Mary Beth picks up her tray and waves at two girls at a table across the room. They gesture and point to an empty chair next to them. "If you don't know, you're the only one in school who doesn't. Even Mrs Scott in the office says you two are a cute couple. That's exactly what she said. A cute couple."

Mary Beth skitters away, laughing, and Cameron slips into her chair.

"What's the joke?"

"Oh, Mary Beth just has the giggles again," I tell him, hoping my blush has faded. "What did your mom say?"

When he smiles, he dazzles me. His teeth are white and even and his skin always looks tanned. Even his dark blue eyes shine. "I'm in," he says, and he throws his arm around my shoulders, pulling me close to him.

"Go for it, Cameron!" a boy shouts. "She's giving hugs today."

"What's he talking about?" Cameron says softly. "Oh, heck, who cares!"

He kisses me then, right in front of everybody, and even though my ears are ringing, I can hear the kids cheer.

I push Cameron away reluctantly. "You're making me feel like an idiot," I complain.

"I'm the idiot. I forgot to pick up something to eat, and now I'm starving."

I push my sandwich towards him. "Take this. I'm so excited I can't eat. You're going to be in Seattle!"

Cameron puts down the sandwich after only one bite. "Why don't we dance? Come on! Get up and dance with me."

"If you want to live long enough to go to music school, you'd better quit this," I warn him, but I'm laughing, too.

He settles down to eat then, and I look around. Everyone is still staring at us. I suddenly feel shy and foolish.

We're a "thing," Cameron and I. People know we're going together.

"Hey!" Cameron says. "I almost forgot. Happy day before your birthday."

I look at my watch. "In less than twenty-four hours, I'll have my licence and we'll be on our way to the farm."

"What if it rains?"

"It won't dare rain," I say. "Nothing can go wrong tomorrow."

"You're right. Tomorrow is going to be the day of days. You get your licence and then we're over the bridge to the farm, ta-ra."

I think suddenly of the cave where fairies and shooting stars and talking caterpillars are born. I shiver and sit up straighter, telling myself that it's all right to think about the cave. Cameron is my star and maybe I'm a fairy princess. We'll keep the talking caterpillars for pets.

But the dark is born there, too.

I'll sweep it away with a magic broom, I tell myself quickly.

"Are you sure you aren't hungry?" Cameron asks.

"I'm sure."

"Then let's go out and walk around the school. The rain's stopped. I'll tell you what I'm going to bring to the picnic."

We walk out hand in hand into the cool April day. The sky is pale blue, washed with thin white clouds — except in the north. In the direction of the farm, the sky is stained dark. The wind comes from there, a damp, weak wind that chills me to the bone.

"It's clearing up," Cameron says. "See? I told you so."

He doesn't see the dark.

▩ ELEVEN ▩

"Happy birthday, Catherine!"

My mother wakes me at eight o'clock, opening my door and carrying in breakfast on a tray.

I sit up, surprised and delighted. "Wow. I never expected this."

She sets the tray in front of me and steps back to admire it. "Well, this is your birthday even though we're not celebrating officially until tomorrow. So I decided to make a special breakfast for you and give you your present from your father and me. You start eating and I'll be right back."

I am looking at strawberry waffles, Canadian bacon, and coffee, and my mouth waters. There's even a rose, a small one in a tall silver bud vase. A silver napkin ring holds the napkin, and I see my initials on that and on the vase, too. I realize that my mother planned this whole thing, and my eyes fill with tears.

She is back, carrying a large package. "You can open it when you've finished eating," she tells me as she goes out.

I eat the best breakfast I've ever had, and when I've finished I put the tray on the floor and pick up the package.

Inside the wrapping is a box from a department store in Seattle. I lift the lid and see a beautiful dark blue blazer. Under that is a soft white wool skirt. And under that, another box, a small one.

I open that box and gape at a long strand of pearls. I know they're real. I touch them to my teeth. They grit slightly, like fine sand. Real pearls, and the jacket and skirt I'd admired in the store's thin and elegant catalogue.

"Cat?"

"Come in, Dad." I'm still holding the pearls and smiling.

He is dressed and looking a little better than he did last night. "You like the pearls, do you?"

"They're beautiful, Dad."

He sits down on my rocker. "Well, now, I thought you might like them so I got them out of the safe-deposit box a while back. Your grandmother and Silvie never really cared for pearls."

I look closely at the fragile old clasp and the glowing pearls. "Are you sure you want me to have them? They must be worth a lot."

"Well, now, Cat, they'll be yours someday anyway," he says. "Just like the farm." He gets up out of the rocker and touches the blazer hesitantly. "Your mother has wonderful taste in clothes. Yes, wonderful."

He walks to the door, and suddenly he seems very sad.

"Dad? Are you feeling better?"

"Why, yes, I believe I am."

"Then will you take me for my driving test? You could pick me up at school about noon."

He turns around and looks at me, and his smile is tired, as if he's worn it too long. "Why, of course, Cat. This is a big day for you."

He goes out and closes the door softly behind him, and I scramble into my underwear as fast as I can. I have a red blouse that will be perfect with the blazer and skirt. I pull it on, buttoning it up with quick fingers. Next the skirt, a perfect fit, and then the blazer.

And then I fasten the pearls around my neck.

My long, pale hair is tousled, but what I see in my mirror makes me happy. Cameron's curtains are still closed, so he won't be able to see me before I leave for school to finish decorating the gym.

But that's all right. He'll see me in a few hours.

Aunt Leah's gift is still sitting on my dressing table. I'm tempted to open it now, but then I remember how she loved the farm and my plans to open the box there. I pat it once.

"Later," I tell it. "The day is only beginning."

I'm the first one at the gym. The tables are arranged around three sides of the room, and a stack of paper table covers waits in a box near the door. I start unfolding the first one just as the gym door swings open and Mary Beth and two other girls come in, carrying buckets of spring flowers.

"Wow! You're all dressed up, birthday girl. Are you sure you don't want to come tonight?"

"I've got other plans, remember?"

Mary Beth shakes her head. "I think you're crazy to miss it."

The rest of the committee comes and we start working. By twelve the gym looks great. The boys tied pink and white balloons to the rafters, and they move gently in the draught. For a moment I'm tempted to ask Cameron if he'd like to stop by for a few minutes. When the place is softly lighted and the band is playing, everyone is going to be impressed with the job we've done.

But Cameron and I have plans for our own dance, and there will be another dance here in June, the senior prom.

We'll go to that.

At twelve-fifteen, my good mood vanishes.

Where is my father? I've been standing in front of the school for fifteen minutes. I look up and down the street, wondering why he's late and what direction he'll come from when he finally arrives.

Mary Beth, the last to leave the gym, drives by and stops. "Do you need a lift?"

"My dad will be here any minute," I tell her, hoping I'm right.

I hate waiting for people. I feel conspicuous and awkward, standing on street corners and checking my watch.

Where is he? Has he forgotten already? I reminded him this morning, and he seemed to be paying attention. But there are times when he looks straight at me, nodding and smiling, and doesn't hear a word I say.

Then I remember something I don't want to remember. One Fourth of July weekend, he went away and never told my mother where he was going. He was gone for three days, and if he ever explained to Mother, she never told me.

It's twelve-twenty. He's forgotten me.

I cross the street to the telephone, digging through my purse for change.

I dial our number and wait while the phone rings six times, eight times, ten times.

Is he on his way here?

I look up and down the street. He has to come. He must come because he promised me that he would.

At twelve-thirty, I call Cameron.

"Well, how does it feel to be a legal driver?" he asks.

"I haven't even taken the test yet. I'm at the drugstore across from school. My dad hasn't turned up. Will you go over to my house and see if he's there? And hurry. I'll hang on till you get back."

I wait, hoping no one else comes to use the phone.

My blouse is sticking to my back. It's not that hot — I'm sticky because I'm scared.

Cameron comes back, panting. "He's not there. I climbed the fence and knocked on the back door. It wasn't locked, so I went inside and looked for him, just in case he was really sick. Or something."

Or something. I can feel tears stinging my eyes. "Did you look in his study?"

"I looked all over. He's not there, but his car is in the drive."

I lean my head against the wall next to the phone. "Great. Now what do I do?"

"Wait just a sec," Cameron says. I can hear his voice but I can't make out the words. He must have his hand over the mouthpiece.

"My dad and I will be there in ten minutes tops. We'll take you for your test." He sounds excited. Happy, even.

"No," I tell him. "I can wait and go next week. Or maybe after school some day."

"Hey, we have plans for today, remember? Dad knows we're going out to the farm for a picnic. He says we can use his car."

"No, Cameron. Listen —"

"See you in ten minutes," he interrupts and then hangs up.

I'm wishing there were some way of getting through the next year without actually having to live it. I'll never forgive my father. Not this time.

In ten minutes Mr Fairchild stops his car at the curb

and beckons to me. I get in the back with Cameron, feeling two years old again. This is awful, really awful.

"You don't have to do this, Mr Fairchild."

"I know that." He pulls out into traffic. "But I didn't have anything else to do today except gardening, and I'm tired of that. I see your father out there in his garden all the time, pottering away. I wish I had his love of the green and growing things. It's all hard work to me."

He's talking too much and I know why. He's seen my father's crazy, crooked garden. He's seen my father, period. Lately it hasn't been a very pleasant sight.

If I live through this, I will never ask for anything again, I tell God. I haven't prayed since January, when I asked God to make my father well. He didn't, so I suppose He isn't listening now, either.

I wish I had never called Cameron. It would have been better to have waited until another day. We could go on a picnic any time.

"Are you nervous?" Cameron asks.

"Don't be nervous!" Mr Fairchild booms from the front seat.

"I'll try," I say. My hands are clenched so tightly that my fingernails have gouged my palms.

"It will all be over in a few minutes, and then you kids can take off for your picnic. Just promise me you won't wreck my new car." He laughs loudly. "I'm just joking, Catherine. I know I can trust you."

I look at Cameron for help, but he is watching out of his window.

"Mr Fairchild, I don't think I should use your car."

"Nonsense! Rubbish! Cars are supposed to be used. I won't hear another word about it."

"Believe him," Cameron whispers. "If you don't use the car, you'll never hear the end of it."

I slump in my seat, hating myself.

"You look nice," Cameron says. "The jacket's new, isn't it?"

"Birthday present," I say numbly.

"What about the pearls?"

"Dad gave them to me. They belonged to the wife of the St John who was the real farmer. My great-grandmother."

Cameron touches them with one finger. "Gee," he says, impressed. He digs through his pocket and comes up with the silver watch. I can hear it ticking.

"You carry it?" I ask, surprised.

"Well, now, I thought I might." He sounds so much like my father that we both start laughing.

"That's it! Stay cheerful, because the worst is yet to come," Mr Fairchild calls out, laughing with us.

Cameron and I reach for each other's hands. It's going to be all right, I tell myself. Somehow, everything always turns out all right, doesn't it?

The queue at the State Patrol office is long enough to discourage anyone. I stand at the end of it, flanked by Fairchild men.

"Smile," Mr Fairchild whispers. "You don't want them to think that you're going to try faking it."

The people nearest us hear him and grin. He looks around proudly, and from the corner of my eye I see Cameron, watching me watching him.

An hour passes, but my turn comes at last. Cameron and Mr Fairchild give me thumbs-up and I back the Fairchild car out of the parking place, with a State Patrol officer sitting beside me. "Relax," he says.

It's over in fifteen minutes. "Practise parking, kid," the officer says. "You're a little stiff, but you'll do."

I'm so excited I can't even remember much of what happened, except that I got two chances at parking since I spoiled the first one by coming to a stop three feet from the kerb. I won't tell anyone that part, I decide.

I march back inside the office with the Fairchilds, father and son, right behind me. We stand in line again until I have my picture taken, and at last the ordeal is over.

Mr Fairchild flips me the car keys. "Drive me home, will you? I'm tired and I want a beer."

"Yea!" Cameron yells. "We're on our way!"

I let Mr Fairchild off in front of his house. He leans back into the car and says, "Have a good time, little girl. And happy birthday."

Cameron walks up the path with him, and they disappear into the house. Cameron is back out again, carrying a picnic basket and a package wrapped in pink paper and silver ribbons. His father follows with an ice chest, and they put all the stuff in the boot.

I remember Aunt Leah's present, and when Cameron gets into the car beside me, I say, "I have to stop by my house. My Aunt Leah sent me a gift and I want to open it at the farm."

"Do I know Aunt Leah?" Cameron asks.

"Aunt Leah of the ten necklaces and jade bracelet. You remember. Every Christmas and birthday I get something fabulous from her."

"Why wait till you get to the farm?"

"Because she loves the farm. Because I promised myself I would open the gift there."

I stop the car in front of my house. Now I remember all over again how my father left me standing on a street corner on my birthday, and a knot of anger tightens in my chest.

"I'll be right back," I tell Cameron.

When I open the front door I know that my father has come back from wherever he was, because I can hear him in his study. He is talking to himself.

"I can't stand this, Sheila. I can't stand this any more."

I burst in the study door, angrier than I have ever been and see him holding a photograph. He drops it upside down on his desk, but it doesn't matter. Right now I don't care.

"Where were you?" I shouted at him. "How could you let me stand there waiting so long? Were you with Sheila? Is she more important to you than I am? Than Mother is?"

"Why, now, Cat —"

"Don't 'why now' me any more. Can't you ever just come out and say what you want to say? You could have told me you didn't want to take me for my test. I would have made some other arrangements. But instead, you let me find out for myself that I'm not important enough for you to remember."

He stands up, reaching for me, his mouth working in a strange way. I think he is going to cry, and I am furious with him. I run up the stairs and slam my bedroom door behind me. I expect him to follow, but he doesn't.

Why am I here? Oh yes, the present from Aunt Leah. I grab it and run back downstairs, passing the study door. I don't look in. I don't want to see him.

When I open the front door, I see Cameron standing outside the car, looking at the house.

"What's the matter? I could hear you clear out here."

"Never mind. I don't want to think about it. Let's go out to the farm."

"Right," he says quickly.

I head out of town, rolling down my window to let the wind blow my hair. Cameron turns on the radio and finds a station we both like.

Anger peels off me in layers. We're only a few blocks from home when I realize that even though we're late, we're still heading for our picnic, and the weather is beautiful. Why should I let my day be spoiled by anything?

But when we pass over the bridge, I cross my fingers.

❖ TWELVE ❖

The afternoon sun warms the old back porch. I sit down and breathe deeply.

The air smells of sweet grass and apple blossoms. The pink and white petals gleam against the cloudless sky where the swallows glide. Here, in this place, I am glad to be alive.

Cameron comes back from his second trip to the car, this time carrying Aunt Leah's package and his gift.

"Open your presents before we eat," he says.

"Whose birthday is this?"

He shoves the package at me. "You know you want to see what's in it."

I pull off the wrapping paper and open the box.

Inside, on top of white tissue, is a folded note.

"Dear Cat," I read. "I found this in Mexico. They call it a wedding dress, but I think it's just right for a dance. Think of me, kiddo, and remember how much I've loved you. Leah."

I lift up the tissue and pull out the dress, holding my breath. There's so much material that in order to see the dress I have to stand up and let it unfold in front of me. The hem falls to my ankles.

"It's great!" Cameron exclaims.

The dress is a pale cream colour, made of rows of ribbon and lace stitched together. The skirt is full — yards and yards of delicate lace and embroidered ribbon shimmer when I move. The top has a low square neck and tiny gathered sleeves looped with more embroidered ribbons.

"Maybe we should go to the school dance tonight," Cameron says. "You're going to look wonderful in that."

"We're having our own dance, remember? I'll wear it here, later on." I fold the dress back into the box, but I leave the lid off because I want to be able to see it.

Cameron hands me the box with the silver ribbons. "This is from my folks."

"That was nice of them." I sit down and open it. Inside is a camera and several packs of films, the kind that develops instantly.

"I told them I was sure you didn't have one," Cameron says. "I was right, wasn't I?"

"Yes, and I've wanted one for a long time. I can't believe it. This is wonderful."

"And here's one more," Cameron says, taking a slim package out of the picnic basket. "I got it for you when I thought I'd be leaving in the fall, but maybe you can use it anyway. Or maybe you won't like it. Open it and see."

He has given me a gold fountain pen. I turn it over and over, studying it. He remembered that I would rather use a fountain pen than a ball point, and he's given me the prettiest one I ever saw.

"I'll write to you with this even if you don't go any farther than Seattle. I'll write to you tomorrow."

He bends down and kisses me quickly. "Happy birthday. And now can we eat? I'm starving."

He's brought fried chicken and potato salad and plastic containers of pickles and olives.

"I've never been this hungry," I tell him.

"Good. I brought enough for two meals, just in case we decide to stay here instead of going to Seattle for dinner. If you don't mind leftovers, that is."

"I love leftovers, and I don't want to go to Seattle today. Let's stay here until dark."

Cameron nods, his mouth full of chicken.

I want the day to last forever. If I could stop time, I would stop it right here, at this moment, sitting in the warm sun in the place I love best in the whole world, with Cameron sitting next to me and the birds in the orchard calling to each other. If I don't think about yesterday and don't think about tomorrow, I can keep safe inside this day.

We eat and afterwards take pictures of each other,

watching our images appear like magic. We take pictures of the trees and the wildflowers and a mother duck leading her babies to the water's edge.

The sun slides down behind the trees. When the afternoon is over and evening begins, Cameron takes out my great-grandfather's watch and tells me the time.

"May I take you up to the porch to dinner, Lady Catherine?" he says, smiling in a wicked way.

"I would love to go to dinner with you, Lord Cameron," I answer, and I curtsy.

We walk back to the house, arm in arm. The breeze is shaking petals loose from the apple trees and some are caught in Cameron's dark hair.

Soon we will dance, I think. We, the last of the April dancers. And we'll come back next year and the year after that. And someday I'll live here, and every spring I'll give a party and invite everyone to dance in my orchard.

But when they've all gone home, Cameron and I will dance alone with blossoms in our hair.

I think of my father and I'm not angry any more.

The sun has gone down. After we eat, Cameron carries the remains of our picnic out to the car and I change into the dress Aunt Leah sent me. Now there is a hush in the orchard. The light wind dies away and the birds are silent. I hear Cameron's footsteps as he walks back around the house.

I look up and he holds out his hands to me.

"You don't look real, standing there," he says.

"You look like something I've dreamed up when I'm lonely for you."

I slide my arms around his neck. "When are you lonely for me?"

He bends his head and kisses my neck. "I'm lonely for you when you're out of sight."

We walk together towards the orchard. I'm barefoot again and the grass whispers against my feet and tugs at the hem of my long skirt.

Without speaking, we move down one row and up the next, until we have passed all the trees and the orchard is dark. Tonight the moon hangs pale and cool over the house.

Cameron stops and takes both my hands. "Your pearls shine in the moonlight," he says softly. "They're the same colour as your hair. Lady, will you dance with me?"

I nod, and he begins to turn, holding both my hands. I lean back, looking up at the sky. Cameron whirls us down the centre of the orchard until we reach the pond.

"Cat," he says softly, urgently, "are you my girl?"

"Oh, yes," I tell him.

We look at each other while the night grows dark and cold around us. The wind has returned, whispering in the trees and disturbing the reeds by the water. I shiver suddenly, uncontrollably.

"What's wrong?" he asks.

I'm afraid, and I don't know why. "It's getting cold."

"Do you want to go?" There is disappointment in his voice.

"I'm sorry," I whisper.

The dark has come.

The dark.

I am warmer in the car, wearing my blazer over the dress my aunt gave me. Cameron talks restlessly.

"We could still go to a movie if you like," he says finally.

"Yes." I like the idea. We could see something to make us laugh. Something silly and noisy.

A few cars pass us, going in the other direction. Headlights approach, flare in my eyes, and flash past. The bridge is coming up, and I cross my fingers automatically. My hands are cold.

We pass over it, and I let out the breath I was holding.

"Hey!" Cameron says. "There's your dad's car!"

I see it just as we pass it. It's parked on the wrong side of the road, halfway in the ditch. I slam on the brakes, and we swerve to the side of the road.

"Are you sure?" I don't want to believe what I saw.

"I think so. Yes, it's his car."

We are out of the car and running before I really grasp what is happening. My shoes slip on gravel — Cameron is ahead of me. He pulls open the door on the passenger side.

He looks back at me. "He's not here."

I stare in the windscreen. The headlights from a passing car light up the inside of my father's car for a moment. "Where is he?" I ask stupidly.

"Mr St John!" Cameron calls out. "Are you here, Mr St John?" He is looking towards the woods, but I am looking at the bridge.

"Mr St John!" Cameron shouts again.

I walk past him, moving along the shoulder to the bridge. There are no street lights out here, so I can only see the near end of the bridge. I hold my chin up and my arms stiff at my sides. The wind grows colder.

Then I am on the bridge and Cameron is calling my name, but I can't look back. A car is coming — I see the lights far up the highway. In a few moments the headlights will shine on the bridge, and I will see whatever there is to see. I keep walking.

"Cat!" Cameron screams behind me. Gravel crackles under his running feet. "Cat, where are you going?"

The car careers onto the bridge, roaring at me, horn blaring.

I stop. At my feet, I see my father's old gardening shoes, placed neatly side by side. The car rushes past, horn splitting open the night. My skirt whips around my ankles.

I bend down in the dark and pick up my father's ridiculous, dumb, insane shoes and hold them against my chest.

Cameron grabs me from behind.

"What the hell is wrong with you?" he screams at me. "That car nearly hit you!"

I look over the bridge railing and out into the dark.

I won't look down to the gorge and the cave where the fairies and shooting stars and talking caterpillars are born. Where the dark leaks out into the world.

"What have you got there?" Cameron asks, turning me around. "My God," he whispers. "Where did you get them?"

"Here."

He is silent.

"Cameron, look down for me. I can't look down."

"It's too dark to see anything, Cat."

"Cameron, look down!"

"It's too dark. I can't see anything. Do you really think he's down there? In the water? Cat, the river goes too fast. It's too deep. Cat?"

I hug the shoes to my chest, looking out into the eternity that stretches between me and my crazy father.

"Dad?" I call out. "*Daddy!* Answer me, Daddy!"

"Oh, God, Cat. Come away from there. Cat, please."

"Daddy, damn you, answer me right now!"

Another car comes. Light sears me and brakes squeal. I hear Cameron's voice. A woman says, "My God, the poor thing."

Oh, Daddy, damn you, you left me again to wait and wait and not know what's happened.

I lean hard against the bridge railing, lift the shoes up and over my head and throw them as far as I can, out into the dark. A shower of small white balls follows the shoes and I wonder what they are, then realize that my pearls are gone.

Someone touches my shoulder and I shrug off the hand. "Honey, please," a woman says. "Come sit in the car with me. They're going for help."

I turn my head and see a line of headlights now. Where did they come from? I didn't hear the cars.

People are standing at the railing, looking down, murmuring.

"Honey, you're shivering. Come and sit in the car. I've got a thermos of coffee."

"Go away, please."

I turn my head and look out into the dark again. I feel my fingernails break on the railing. I grip harder. The pain tells me this is all real. It's happening.

I am Catherine Silvie St John and today I am sixteen and I killed my father.

I hear sirens whooping and brakes and voices.

"She won't talk to me," the woman says.

Someone wraps a blanket around me and tries to pull my hands from the railing, but I can't let go. Now I can look down and I see lights bobbing on both sides of the gorge.

Cameron is here again, bending my fingers back to get them off the railing.

"Let me alone," I tell him.

"Aw, Cat, for God's sake." He is crying.

But I don't cry. I watch the bobbing lights.

A radio crackles with static nearby. A man says, "What've you got?"

"He's here," a tiny metallic voice sputters.

"How does it look?" the man says.

"Too late," the metallic voice rasps.

"Where?" the man says.

"There's a cave down here," the metal man on the radio croaks. "He washed up in the back of it."

"Oh, no," I say. "No-no-no-no!"

A scream rises up from the dark inside me and I can't stop it. I can't stop it even while they force me down on a stretcher and slide me into the back of the white van that has been waiting in the middle of the bridge.

Cameron's mother has come from somewhere, and she sits beside me in the van. She holds me when the man in the grey jacket speaks into a radio, and she holds me when he pricks my arm with a needle.

She is still holding me when the dark swallows me up.

❈ THIRTEEN ❈

I can hear someone eating.

"Well, Catherine. You're awake."

Grandma St. John sits next to my hospital bed, eating jam doughnuts from a bag. She is wearing her "church" dress, a dark blue silk, and it's buttoned wrong. And she is wearing pink satin bedroom slippers. She must have slicked back her curly white hair with water. Underneath, the frizz peeps through the straightened strands.

Altogether, I decide, she looks like an unmade bed, and I wonder why. And wonder what she is doing here. And wonder what I'm doing here.

I remember, and the memory of last night hits me in the stomach, knocking out my breath.

"I rushed off as soon as your mother called me this morning," she says calmly. "I was getting ready for the early church service. On the way here I got my breakfast from that little bakery a few blocks from my apartment. Help yourself, Catherine."

I think she is crazy. She is sitting there gobbling jam doughnuts and her son is dead.

"Where's Mother?"

"Silvie went home two hours ago," she says, patting her mouth with a paper napkin. "She was exhausted, sitting here all night." She bites into another doughnut. "You've been asleep," she adds unnecessarily.

The room is painted yellow. An empty bed is by the window, and I have a view of a yellow wall. I see two handprints near the ceiling, and I wonder who made them and why. Someone must have climbed up there and pressed her dirty hands against the wall. Why would anyone do that? Maybe this is the place where they put crazy people.

"The doctor said you could leave at noon," Grandma says. "It's a quarter to twelve now. You might as well get dressed."

I remember that the doctor listened to my heart — probably to see if it was broken. Was my mother here then? I can't remember that.

I get out of bed and take my clothes from the little cupboard next to the bathroom door. Grandma looks up once, then gobbles her way through the rest of the doughnuts.

"That's a pretty dress," she says finally, as I slip Aunt Leah's gift over my head. "You're like your mother — you know what looks good on you."

I don't tell her that Aunt Leah gave me the dress, because she would change her mind about it.

"I'm going to feel silly leaving here in a long dress," I mumble.

"Maybe no one will notice," Grandma says.

We are both crazy. My father is dead and we are worrying about what I'll look like when I leave the hospital.

I don't have a comb. My hair is tangled, and Grandma doesn't have a comb, either. She hands me my new blazer and then trots out of the room. She returns, followed by a nurse who is as fat as she is. The nurse's face is scarlet. Grandma has that effect on people.

"The doctor hasn't signed the release yet," the nurse says.

"Try not to be silly," Grandma says. "Are you ready, Catherine?"

"Yes, Grandma."

"Then let's go home."

The nurse is standing in the doorway, and Grandma tries to bump past her. They look like two sailing ships at war in a bathtub.

"She can't leave yet," the nurse says sharply.

"Get out of my way, you idiot," Grandma cries, flapping her large handbag at the nurse. "I'm taking my granddaughter home right now."

The nurse backs off and Grandma sails past, victorious.

"She has to leave in a wheelchair. Hospital rules," the nurse protests.

Grandma stops and turns around, glaring at me. "Can you walk, Catherine?" she demands.

"Of course. Yes, I can walk." I am embarrassed. People passing in the hall have stopped to stare.

"Then walk, girl." Grandma sails on down the hall and I rush after her, a little rowing boat bouncing in the wake of the Spanish Armada.

We go down together in the lift. As we get near the front entrance, Grandma stops and digs through her huge handbag. She comes up with keys on a gold key ring.

"Here, Catherine."

"You want me to drive, Grandma?" I ask. I don't feel like driving. I've lost my purse somewhere (I don't dare wonder where) so I don't have my licence. It seems very important that I don't break any laws now. Catherine St John, shot full of sedatives and driving without a licence. What would everyone say? My legs shake under me.

"I thought you'd want to drive," Grandma says, surprised.

"I feel sick," I tell her. "If you don't mind . . ."

She folds her fat fingers around the keys and sighs. "I'll never understand you young people," she complains. Her faded eyes fix on me. "Well, come on, Catherine. There's no sense in standing here all day."

I follow her out of the door and up the street, shivering in the damp wind that stirs the flowers in the hospital flower beds. Grey clouds hang over the town, blotting out the light, and I smell rain in the air.

Grandma stops beside a new sports car, bright red. She sticks a key in the lock, and I see the initials CSS over the door handle.

"Get in, child. I'll never see why you youngsters like cars like this. The seats are impossible and there's no leg room."

Whose car is this, I wonder.

"Well? Do you like it, child? Did I pick the right one? Silvie said you'd like it, so I went ahead and had your initials put on the doors. That's why I couldn't get it until yesterday afternoon. Well? What do you think?"

Both of us stand there with the car door open, gaping at the leather seats. Her words arrange themselves in my mind, and I understand. This is my car.

"Grandma," I say weakly. "It's beautiful."

"Then get in," she snaps. "We can't stand out here being gawped at by these peculiar people."

No one is looking at us. I get in, folding my long skirt carefully around my legs. Grandma toddles around the front of the car and gets into the driving seat.

"This seat will cripple me," she says as she starts the car. "I thought I'd have to stop a dozen times on the way here."

"I'm sorry, Grandma."

My father is dead, I think, and we are very careful not to mention that unpleasant fact. I'm glad, because if she says the words aloud I'll be crushed under the stone that sits on my chest.

We drive down sleepy streets, and Grandma complains about her back and the car and the weather. I sit and pleat my long lace and ribbon skirt between my numb fingers. We are playing some sort of game. I don't know the rules but I must play, because if the game comes apart we'll have to talk about last night.

"I ordered a cake for you, Catherine," she says. "But I forgot it at home. Can you imagine? I don't know what's getting into me these days. I'd forget my head if it weren't fastened to my neck."

"That's all right, Grandma."

"Well, it's not all right. You should have a cake. Everyone should have a special cake on her sixteenth birthday."

"I don't mind, Grandma."

We are driving down my block now. Grandma stops the car in front of my house. I see my mother's car in the drive. But not my father's.

"Here we are, Catherine," Grandma says.

And then she puts her head down on the steering wheel and sobs. I am horrified. I don't know what to do. I pat her arm helplessly.

"It was the war," she cries. "It was that goddamn war."

My hands snap together in shock and I can't loosen my fingers. Grandma's shoulders are shaking. Tears drip into her lap.

"War?" I ask, stupefied.

I don't think she hears me. She is talking to God or the devil. She is explaining something to someone.

"I didn't even know him when he came back. It was that war!"

"But he wasn't wounded in the war. He told me so, a long time ago." I don't understand what she is talking about. My father never talked about the war. Once I asked him if he had been in Vietnam and he told me he had. When I asked him if he had been hurt, he said no. He looked straight into my eyes and said nothing had happened.

He is dead because he couldn't find a job, and because of Sheila, but mostly because of me. But I can't say those things. My mouth won't open, and my tongue is stuck to the roof of my mouth.

"I can't let your mother see me like this," Grandma says finally, raising her head and scrubbing away tears with the backs of her hands. "We have to be strong, don't we, Catherine? Yes, we have to be strong."

"Yes, Grandma."

We go into the house, a dumpy old lady in a blue silk dress and pink satin slippers and her only granddaughter, who is carrying out the new family tradition of wearing clothes that are completely ridiculous for the occasion.

I can smell burned bacon.

The living room curtains are still closed, holding in the smell. I walk through the dining room to the kitchen, Grandma clucking behind me like a distressed hen.

I don't see Mother anywhere. The kitchen is an incredible mess. A pan containing blackened strips of bacon sits in the sink, on top of a cracked bowl of raw eggs. A dishcloth is draped over the edge of the bowl, soaked with the eggs. Another bowl has been broken on the counter — slabs of glass are scattered in spilled orange juice. The juice jug is on its side. Orange juice is puddled on the floor. A fork is on the floor in front of the sink, an opened loaf of bread on the small table, the Sunday paper scattered under the chairs. Some of the cupboard doors are open and the refrigerator door is ajar. The kitchen phone is off the hook and making strange noises.

Grandma replaces the phone. "Go change your clothes, Catherine," she says briskly. "I'll have lunch on the table before you can wink an eye."

The house is quiet, except for the racket Grandma makes as she starts to clean the kitchen. I pass Father's open study door and go up the stairs to my room. My parents' door is closed. I hear nothing behind it.

My room is bathed in pale light. I stand at the window, looking across to Cameron's window. His house looks quiet — occupied but quiet. Cameron is not in his room.

My purse is sitting on my desk. I open it and find the gold pen Cameron gave me right on top. The camera is next to the purse, along with a stack of pictures. My white skirt and red blouse are hanging over the back of my rocker.

Someone was here — Cameron or his father. I

don't care. I strip off the dress my aunt Leah gave me and throw it on the bed.

In the shower, I let water pour over my hair for a long time before I shampoo it. My face feels so stiff that I wonder why it doesn't chip when I wash it. When I get out of the shower, I forget to turn off the water. I go back and turn the taps the wrong way before I turn them the right way.

My jeans feel too big. I look in the mirror at my stiff face and wet hair. The sweatshirt I pull on doesn't look right.

What do sixteen-year-old girls wear on a day like this? How do we act and what do we say? Is there a book somewhere that has all that information in it?

I sit down on the bed and look at my very own yellow walls. No handprints on them. Not yet.

The phone rings in my room and all over the house. I don't answer because I don't know who is calling and since I haven't read the book on suitable behaviour the day after you kill your father, I won't know the right things to say. The phone stops ringing — Grandma must have answered it in the kitchen. Maybe she knows what to say on a day like this.

I can see myself in the mirror from where I sit. I don't like what I see, so I get up from the bed and open the top drawer of my desk.

I take out the scissors and cut off my long wet hair.

Grandma calls us for lunch. Mother and I meet in the hall. She is wearing her silver robe.

"Are you all right, Catherine?" she asks.

"I think so. Are you all right?"

"I'll be fine." Her eyelids are swollen and pink.

She doesn't comment on my hair.

We walk downstairs together. The kitchen is clean again. Grandma has fixed tuna fish sandwiches and chicken noodle soup. A pot of tea sits in the centre of the table.

"Tea, Silvie? Catherine?" Her old hands have brown spots on them, and the skin is soft and wrinkled. She is trembling.

"Yes, thank you," Mother says as she sits down, spine erect.

"I'll have tea, too," I tell Grandma.

"Tea is so civilized," Grandma says as she pours the steaming, clear liquid into the bone china cups.

And so are we, I think.

When all else fails, the St John women are civilized. Of course, we are also crazy today.

Maybe I'll have to write that book myself.

"Catherine," Grandma says, "I wish you'd find a better hairdresser."

◼ FOURTEEN ◼

DEAR SHEILA

I looked for you at my father's memorial service today, but I didn't see anyone I didn't recognize.

You must know he's dead — it was in the paper. "Son of Prominent Historian Plunges to His Death." Most of the article was about Grandpa St John.

The minister talked about the end of suffering, but I stopped listening. I was thinking about the people who came — wondering where you were and why I never noticed before that my father didn't have any friends.

God didn't show up either. Let's face it — he's never around when you need him.

But then, neither are you.

The neighbours cried and so did my friends, but the St John women sat looking at the floor. We didn't shed so much as one tiny tear between the three of us. Afterwards we shook hands with everyone, patted their backs, hugged the ones who cried hardest, and told everyone they'd feel better soon.

I wasn't sure why we were the ones doing all the comforting, but that's how it was.

My father was cremated and the urn holding his ashes can be seen in that big stone building at the cemetery, if you're interested.

Sincerely,

CATHERINE ST JOHN

I open the top drawer of my desk, adding the letter to my collection. Then I get dressed for school.

This will be my first day back. Mother is staying home for a few more days, but there's no reason for me to stay here in the dead dusty quiet any more. Well, there's one reason, but I can take care of that before I leave.

Mother is still in her room. She sleeps a lot. I glide downstairs and open the door to my father's study. Mother said she was going to be "sorting out papers" soon. I'm not certain what papers she's talking about, but just in case she means the stuff in my father's desk, I'd better get to it first.

It bothers me — being in this room. It seems to be full of my father. I don't mean his stuff. I mean my *father*. He spent a lot of time in here last winter after he lost his job. The room is tired and confused.

I scratch through the jumbled papers on top of the desk. There is no photograph here except the framed one of Mother and me. The picture my father held was unframed. I open the middle drawer and see a dozen pill bottles crammed in the back. I read the labels and count the tranquillizers and antidepressants. The prescription dates go back several years. He had them but he didn't take them. And no one told me anything. So what else is new?

I go through all the drawers, and the only photos I find are old ones of my father and his brother when they were children and a wedding picture of James and Leah, along with another picture taken at the same wedding. That picture was of my parents. They were both smiling.

Perhaps my father had Sheila's picture with him when he died. I don't know what happens to the things people are carrying when they jump off bridges.

I close the study door quietly and leave the house. The brilliant sunshine suprises me. It's Friday, the first Friday in May. Winter is only in my head.

At school, Suzy is standing by her locker when I walk by. She called me several times this week, so I stop to thank her. Her eyes are swollen and red and her nose is running.

"What's wrong?"

She slams her locker door shut. "Charlie's mother. She's so awful she ought to be taken out and run over a couple of times."

I agree, but I'm surprised to see Suzy so angry. "What's she done?"

Suzy sags against her locker. "I can't bother you with my problems at a time like this. What are you doing back in school, anyway? No one expected you to show up for weeks."

Was I wrong coming back now? Maybe it looks like I didn't care about my father. How long is someone supposed to stay home?

I shake my head irritably. No matter what I do, it seems to be wrong. "You can't hide from the world forever," I say. I've found that the most stupid remarks are taken as profound observations during life's especially horrible times.

Suzy pats my arm. "You're awfully brave. I couldn't have stood up to all this as well as you have."

I have to get her off this subject. "Tell me what Charlie's mother did."

"She told Charlie that if he takes me to his senior prom they're going to change their minds about letting him go to Europe in July. I didn't want him to go anyway, but he wants to, and three of his friends are going, and I don't know what he's going to decide."

I know, but there's no point in hurting her feelings. "Parents can put a lot of pressure on kids," I tell her. Big news flash.

"I know," she moans. "She's such a lousy snob. She thinks she's better than anyone else in this town. Oh, Cat, what am I going to do?"

What can I tell her? She'd never do what she should do and that's tell Charlie she never wants to see him again. Charlie and his mother are an institution. He doesn't take a breath unless she gives him permission. She's always holding treats just out of reach — it's like someone teasing a dog. "Jump, Charlie, or you don't get to go to Europe. Roll over, Charlie, or you won't get that car."

"Try not to worry, Suzy. Things will turn out the way they're going to turn out."

I see Cameron coming towards me. He's smiling as if he hadn't been sitting in our garden until after dark last night. And every other night since . . . my birthday.

"You made it," he says, leaning down to brush my cheek with his lips.

"Sure." Last night we sat on the lawn swing holding hands, not talking. My mother watched us through the window. His mother telephoned to tell him to come home.

We say goodbye to Suzy, and Cameron walks me to my first class. I try to ignore the stares I'm getting. Some people rush at me, their faces twitching as smiles change places with frowns. I'm sorry they feel so awkward.

"How *are* you?" they cry. "I was thinking about you." "I was going to call you." "Can I do anything?"

I put on my Brave Smile and nod my way past them. Cameron squeezes my hand.

When I walk into my first class, the kids stop talking for a second and then start in again. Or is it my imagination?

Now I wish I'd stayed home, behind the closed curtains in the dusty living room. Next to the room with all the pills that somebody should have been taking but didn't.

At lunch-time, Mary Beth and I eat on the lawn in front of the school. I keep my back to the place where I stood last Saturday, waiting for my father to come.

Mary Beth wipes her fingers on a paper napkin. "Are you sure you feel okay? Should you have come back to school?"

"I didn't know what else to do."

My honesty hurts her. Her eyes fill with tears. "I wouldn't know what to do, either."

We sit in silence, watching the birds on the lawn.

"I'm going home," I say suddenly. I don't know where the words came from. Mary Beth is no more surprised than I am.

She blinks. "Oh. You want me to go with you?"

I shake my head. "If you see Cameron, tell him I left," I say.

"Sure. And you take it easy," she calls after me.

Mother is cleaning the living room when I get home. She's washed her hair, I see. But there are even more lines on her face today than there were yesterday.

"Please sit down a minute, Catherine," she says. She doesn't ask why I'm home early. With quick, nervous fingers she loops up the vacuum cleaner cord. "I've got something to tell you."

I sit down on the couch, perching on the edge of a cushion like a suspicious bird. Now what's wrong?

"I've decided to sell this house," she says.

I never expected that. My mouth is open. "Why? Where are we going to live?"

She sits down in the chair opposite me. "It's too big for the two of us. I can get a good price for it, and we'll need the money."

"But . . . but he hasn't even been dead for a week!"

She stares at me and I see her swallow hard. "We'd been talking about it for several weeks. His severance pay would have run out pretty soon, and we couldn't have afforded to stay here. Now — well, I'm afraid I really don't have a choice."

"Then we'll move to the farm!" I blurt.

She shakes her silvery head. "He left the farm to

you, Catherine, but I think you should sell it. You'll need the money for college some day. We can't live there anyhow. It's too big, too run-down. It would cost every cent I have to fix it up. I'll find an apartment somewhere."

She has said two things that crash over me. My father gave me the farm and we are going to be living in an apartment. I can only deal with one at a time.

"I hate apartments. I don't want to live in one."

She looks down at the carpet. "I'll find a nice one, you'll see. And it's only for a year or so. You'll be living in Seattle when you start college. In a dormitory. Or maybe a sorority house. It won't matter to you then where I'm staying."

"It's too soon." My lips are numb. "I'm not ready to move away from here." And Cameron. I'll never be ready to move away from Cameron.

"I'll rent the house first. It will take a while to sell. Probably most of the summer. Then again maybe not."

She's beginning to sound like my father. "Which is it?" I ask harshly. "Most of the summer or then again maybe not?"

I'm hurting her and I don't want to. I have to be careful, because I hurt my father so badly I killed him. Catherine the Killer-mouth. Every word a knife.

"I understand how upset you are," she says. "I knew you'd feel this way. So I've worked out some plans to make it easier for you."

"What? A general anaesthetic?"

"Your aunt Leah is back in San Diego," she says,

ignoring my sarcasm. "I talked to her on the phone this morning. I'm sending you to stay with her for the summer."

For a moment I can barely breathe. "But I haven't seen her since I was six years old! I hardly know her."

Mother stands up. My interview is obviously over. "You'll love San Diego," she tells me. "And you'll enjoy Leah. She can be lots of fun."

"And if she isn't lots of fun?" I shout at her back as she walks out of the room. "What do I do if she's not lots of fun?"

She stops in the doorway. Her face sags and her eyes look through me. "This will be best. I've made you a reservation for a flight tomorrow evening."

"But I'm not out of school yet!"

"Your principal says it will be all right, everything considered."

I don't believe this. This can't be happening.

She's had a busy morning, I think bitterly. She made plans to get rid of both the house and me.

Well, I'm not going. I'll think of something. She'll come to her senses by tomorrow. This won't happen because it can't. What will I do without Cameron for a whole summer?

Why is she doing this to me?

She found out what I did. She knows that I yelled at my crazy father and he killed himself.

I curl up in a ball on the couch, with my chin on my knees and my eyes squeezed shut. But I don't cry. I don't do that any more.

✹ FIFTEEN ✹

I sit in my room, watching Cameron's window for some sign that's he's come home from school. I can't think straight. Every time I try to sort all of this out, I expect my brain to start buzzing and blow up.

I see Cameron pass in front of his window, and I snatch up the phone.

My mother is using it. She's telling a client that his offer is accepted. You'd never know from her voice that terrible things have been happening around here.

I stand by the window, waiting for Cameron to look up and see me. He always does.

At last he looks across me. He picks up his phone and waves it in the air.

How can I leave him?

I lift the receiver again. She's hung up at last. Cameron answers the moment his phone starts to ring.

"Why did you go home?" he asks. "Did something happen?"

"Not at school."

"What's going on?" he asks, but something in his voice warns me that he might already know. He sounds so discouraged.

"Have you heard about it?" I ask.

"Heard about what?" He's being evasive. That's not like him. Cameron is always a truth-teller.

"About my mother wanting me to go to California? You already know, don't you? Everybody knows but Cat."

He doesn't say anything. He's standing there, the phone dangling from one hand and the receiver pressed against his ear. He's staring at me.

"It's okay," I tell him. "I'm not mad at you. I guess you couldn't let on that our mothers have been gossiping over the back fence again. Right?" I'm giving him every let-out I can think of, because I can't bear being angry with him right now. I have to have somebody.

"What are you talking about? What do you mean, you're going to California? I didn't know about that."

He's just standing there, staring at me. He didn't know, and I've shocked him.

"My mother told me when I got home. She's sending me to stay with my aunt Leah for the summer. She thinks she is, anyway. I've got to think of something. Help me."

"She's doing it because of me," he says.

"What do you mean?"

"My mother came home from work early to talk to me. Your mother called her today and said she doesn't think we should be seeing each other so much." Cameron isn't whispering any more. He's talking loud enough for his mother to hear, and I'm feeling sick.

"Did she tell you I'm supposed to go to California?"

He clears his throat. "No. She didn't say anything about that. Just that I'm to stay away from you, because you're so upset and this isn't the time for you to be getting involved, Mom said. That's what your mom told her. And my mom agreed." He shouts the last part.

We face each other across our gardens and a fence that is growing higher every moment.

I hear a click on the line. My mother says, "Catherine, I have to use the phone. Would you mind hanging up?"

"Yes!" I shout. "I would mind very much. I'm having a private discussion and I don't want you eavesdropping."

My mother hangs up. Cameron and I look at each other.

"Tonight," he whispers. "Like last time. Watch for my signal."

I look across at him and nod. Tonight I'll crawl out of my window and he'll meet me at the fence.

We'll work out something.

*   *   *

My clock says five-thirty when Mother calls me. "Catherine! Are you coming down to dinner?"

I open my bedroom door a crack. "No. I'm not hungry."

I wait to see what happens. Time ticks by.

"All right," Mother says with one of her big sighs. "Since you aren't coming down, you might as well start packing the things you'll need for a couple of weeks. I'll send the rest to you after you leave. And while you're at it, you can sort out anything you don't want to keep."

I shut the door.

She means it. I lie down on my bed and look at the ceiling. Something will happen, and I'll still be here in a month, getting ready to go to the senior prom with Cameron.

An hour later, Mother comes to my door. "I brought up these two suitcases for you to use." She drops them on my floor. "You should be able to pack enough clothes in them to last a couple of weeks."

I want to kick the suitcases, but I sit up and ask Mother to listen to me.

"There's nothing more to talk about," she says. "You'll be better off with your aunt for a while. You'll love being there. Just wait and see."

"It's because of Cameron, isn't it?"

She blinks. "That's part of it. This is a difficult time for all of us. And you're too . . . intense about Cameron."

"I don't know what that means. Intense." I know but I'm offended. She's acting as though I'm twelve years old, agonizing over a crush on a football player.

She brushes aside my request for clarification. "His parents agree with me. Cameron has to concentrate on his studies. His music."

"He doesn't start music school until fall," I argue.

She is easing towards the door, looking around my room as if she's taking an inventory. "Did I tell you your plane leaves at seven-fifteen tomorrow night? Why don't you ask Mary Beth and Suzy to come to the airport with us?"

I'm so cold I shiver. "No. I can't leave school now. I don't want to be away from my friends all summer long. Not now, especially."

She looks at me for a long time. "Catherine," she says quietly, "I'm asking you to help me out. I can't stand any more worries. Your father left us with no insurance, very little in the bank, and a pile of bills I'll need years to clear up unless I sell this house. I'm sorry you're upset, but I'm upset, too. And we have to get along as best we can now."

"But why can't I stay here?" I shout. "Why?"

"Because I don't want to have to lie awake at night wondering what you and Cameron are doing!" she shouts. "I don't want to hear you talking to him on the phone and wonder how long it's going to be before you come crying to me that you're pregnant. I don't want —"

"What?" I shout. "How can you say that to me? I've never —"

"Not yet!" she shouts back.

Both of us are panting. We have locked eyes and I don't want to be the first to look away.

How dare she say something like that about me! What's the matter with her that she thinks Cameron and I . . .

I look away first.

"I'm afraid to leave him," I whisper.

"I know."

I raise my gaze, hoping that understanding will have softened her. The Silver Lady looks implacably back at me.

"That's why I'm sending you away. Because you're afraid to leave him. Catherine! I don't want you depending on him for everything. Your father's gone — you're looking for someone to depend on now. I don't want it to be a boy. Especially one you think you're in love with."

She said it. She said what I never could tell Cameron and what he never could tell me.

I go back to my bed and lie down facing the wall. "Go away. I want to be by myself."

Cameron. Help me.

I scratched my leg climbing the pear tree under Cameron's window.

"It's bleeding," he whispers. "Do you want me to get you a plaster?"

"It's all right." I sit on the floor next to his bed and lean against it. I've never been so tired.

Cameron sits in front of me, hands me a glass of cola and an ancient candy bar. His stereo is playing and his door is locked. His parents are asleep — I hope.

"I packed most of the stuff I'll be taking," I whisper. "But I can't go. We have to think of something."

"Did you try talking to her?"

"Of course. But we haven't been talking much this last week and I think I'm out of the habit. Or she's out of the habit of listening. Maybe she never did."

I can't eat the candy, even though I skipped dinner. My stomach is full of this last week and it's making me sick. I lean my head back and close my eyes.

"It seems like a long time," Cameron says softly. "But it's really only three or four months. We can handle three or four months, can't we?"

I haven't been his special girl long enough to know how things are when you're Cameron Fairchild's steady. Can he be away from me for the whole summer without wanting to die?

"I want you to feel better about everything," he says. "You look like a lost little kid. You've got a lost-little-kid haircut even. Maybe if you spent the summer with your aunt you'd be all right again. And I'd come to see you."

"There's nothing wrong with me," I protest. Then my mind catches up with my ears. "You'll come to San Diego? How?"

He shrugs. "I don't know yet. And next fall I'll come home every weekend. Everything will be okay, you'll see."

"But I won't be here then, either. She's selling the house."

Cameron's dark blue eyes are close to mine. His lean face tenses. "What?"

"My mother is selling the house. She says she has to. My father left the farm to me, but she doesn't want to live there. She wants to move to an apartment."

"Here? In Waterford?"

"Maybe. I guess. I don't really know. But we won't be living across the fence from each other any more."

He leans towards me and brushes his lips against mine. "I'll find you, Cat."

I cover my face with my hands. He electrifies me — I want to cry, but I still don't have tears. I reach out for him, and we hold each other without speaking for a long time.

"I promise you, Cat. I'll always find you."

"I hope so."

"Listen, Green Eyes," he whispers in my ear. "Go to California without arguing any more. Go and pretend everything is all right. Maybe she'll let you come back sooner, when she's found an apartment and has a chance to get used to everything."

"Maybe she won't let me come back at all. Maybe she's trying to get rid of me."

He's quiet long enough so that I know he's really thinking about what I said. He shakes his head. "No. She wouldn't do anything like that." He laughs softly. "What would the neighbours think? My mother wouldn't do anything that would make the neighbours talk. You know how they are."

He's right. But I still feel I'm being given away.

"I wonder if she knows about the fight I had with Dad that last day."

"You didn't have a fight with him," Cameron says. "You were mad and you had a good reason. But he didn't argue with you. I heard the whole thing."

"I never gave him a chance to explain. I accused him of spending time with Sheila."

The name slipped out before I could stop it.

"Who's Sheila?" he asks.

"Some woman my dad wrote to and talked about when he was all mixed up. I don't know if it's someone here in Waterford or someone he used to know. But she's been on his mind — she *was* on his mind. A lot."

"Are you trying to tell me that your dad was having an affair or something? That's really crazy, Cat."

I guess it is, but I really don't know why. Maybe because my dad was so broken and vulnerable. There wasn't time in his life for loving anyone — there was only time for him to be afraid.

"Well, there was a woman," I say. "I don't know who, but he called me by her name a couple of times, and I saw a letter he started writing to her."

"That could mean anything. You know how he was getting."

I pull away from him. "Don't. We shouldn't talk about him like that."

"Sorry," he whispers, reaching for me again.

I lean against his chest for a long time, not talking. I keep my eyes closed and Cameron rocks me in his arms.

The radio announcer tell us the time. It's two in the morning. "I have to go home," I whisper. "Cameron, will you come to the airport when I leave?"

"I'll be there. What time?"

"Seven-fifteen tomorrow night. And Mother wants me to ask Suzy and Mary Beth to go, too."

Cameron is thoughtful for a moment. "She won't want me. How about if I find my own way there? If I try to ride with you, she'll toss me out on the freeway."

I laugh with my mouth pressed against his shirt. He smells of good things — clean clothes and soap.

Probably I smell like unshed tears.

He runs his fingers over my short hair. "I'm trying to get used to this. Will you let it grow out again?"

"I don't know why I cut it in the first place. It just seemed like the right thing to do at the time. It'll be grown out partway when I see you in the autumn."

"I'll be seeing you before that," he says against my neck. "Somehow I'll see you before summer is over."

Before summer is over.

He kisses my face and my neck and the palms of my hands. And then he pulls me to my feet.

"I'd better help you back over the fence now, before we get caught." His grin tells me he doesn't care if we get caught — not too much, anyway.

"Wait a second," I say, suddenly remembering something. I take two key rings out of my jeans pocket. "Here. This big one has the farm keys on it. The short fat key is for the barn. Will you cut the grass for me when I'm gone? It belongs to me now and my father . . ."

"I know," he whispers. "I'll take care of it. And I'll check the windows and all."

"And the other keys are for my car. When she sells the house I don't know what she'll do with it. So I want you to keep it for me. I'll tell her tomorrow before I leave. There isn't anything she can do about it — it's my car."

Cameron shakes his head. "I can't do that."

"Cameron, please."

He laughs. "I won't have a licence for another two months. What am I going to do with a car?"

I grin at him. "Wash and polish it, dummy. We both know you drive your dad's car all alone sometimes."

"I'll send you pictures of the car every week so you can see I'm taking good care of it."

"No, send pictures of the farm. Take pictures of the trees and the ducks. I'll be back before the leaves come down, I hope."

Cameron bends his head and kisses me, squeezing me so hard I can't breathe. "Next spring," he says, "we'll dance again. Just you and me."

I try to bury myself in his arms. "Next spring is so far away. Oh, Cameron, it's too far away."

❂ SIXTEEN ❂

The plane gathers speed, and suddenly I realize that it's left the ground. My heart is stone in my chest. I close my eyes against the pain. What if I never see Cameron again?

I'll never see my father again. Does he know his Cat is flying away tonight? Up there in the stars, is he watching? Or is he smiling down on someone who didn't hurt him as much as I did?

The last thing I did before I left was tear up all my letters to Sheila and flush them down my loo. Mother wouldn't be too happy to pack up my news bulletins to Sheila. Maybe she'll find some my father wrote and forgot to mail. Maybe he mailed everything and Mother will have to do something with Sheila's answers.

Part of me is horrified and part of me isn't too awfully sorry that she might learn about Sheila. After all, what kind of mother gives her daughter away?

Mary Beth and Suzy cried at the airport. But I was looking over their shoulders, searching for Cameron. Just before I left I saw him, standing at the far side of the waiting room. He looked at us without smiling. No one saw him but me.

"Good-bye, baby," Mother called. Baby? She hadn't called me that for ten years.

" 'Bye," Mary Beth and Suzy said. "Don't forget to write."

But my eyes were on Cameron. He touched one hand to his heart and then to his lips.

Everything in me yearned towards him. I touched my fingers to my heart and then my lips. And left.

A family is sitting across from me. The daughter, about twelve or thirteen, sits by the window looking out at the mountains below us. Her parents have ordered drinks and a pack of cards, and they are laughing over their game. The father is strong and grizzled, with a heavy beard and laugh lines around his eyes. Papa Bear.

He won't plant crazy crooked gardens in his back yard. Or leave his gardening shoes on a bridge on his daughter's sixteenth birthday. She'll grow up and marry and have children, and he will be a Grandpa. The one everyone turns to when they have a problem.

And his daughter will never say anything to him that is so cruel he'd rather be dead than remember it.

The sky darkens and I soar through the evening.

When the pilot tells us that we are approaching San Diego, I look out and see heaps and strands of glowing, glittering lights, jewels on a black blanket.

The woman next to me leans over me to see out of the window. "That's the most beautiful sight in the world," she says. "No matter where I go, coming home is best."

I wouldn't know.

The plane groans and shudders, and the wings tremble. We drop closer to the lights. Will my aunt remember that I'm coming?

My stomach knots. What if she doesn't remember? What if she never really meant for me to come after all?

And then, Catherine St John, what will you do? Who will be your family?

I am suffocated with fear when I leave the plane. Somewhere in my purse I have Leah's phone number and address. I'll find a phone and call her. Maybe she won't mind that I actually showed up. I'll be awfully good. I'll never argue with her, and I'll make my bed and help out around the house.

I follow Papa Bear and his family through the gate, looking around to see if by chance anyone resembling the photos of Aunt Leah is waiting.

I see her. She's here. Tall, with greying hair pulled back into a knot, the woman from the photos strides towards me, white teeth shining in her tanned face.

"Well, kiddo," she says, "right on time."

She carries one suitcase and I carry the other, and we step out of the airport into a warm, windy night.

"How's your mother?" she asks as she points towards a car nearby.

"She's okay, I guess."

"She sounded like she was hanging in there when I talked to her on the phone. It takes time for something like this to sink in, though."

She puts my baggage in the boot of her car. "I'm glad she agreed to let you come here for the summer. It seemed to me that the last thing either one of you needed was all the confusion of moving at a time like this, but she's positive it's the only way to get herself back in a good financial situation. But what the hell were you supposed to be doing when all this was going on?"

She slams the passenger door after I get into the car and hurries around to the driver's door, opening it and continuing her conversation.

"I hate moving," she barks. Backing up the car takes her attention for a moment. "All that damned packing and cleaning. Trying to find a suitable place for a price that won't leave you eating bread and peanut butter for a year. What did she expect you to do while she was running around looking for an apartment?"

We're on a motorway now, and I look out at the glowing city skyline.

"So I said, 'Silvie, send Cat down to me for the

154

summer. She shouldn't be dragging around behind you, trying to get herself back together and adjust to a new home at the same time. Let me have her,' I said, 'and you sell your house and move if you must. But give the kiddo a break.'"

I can see why Grandma St John and my mother aren't too crazy about Aunt Leah. Grandma especially. She hates to have anyone else do any talking, and Aunt Leah doesn't seem to do anything but talk.

She threads the car quickly through warm, quiet streets and pulls in, at last, beside a dark house.

"Here we are, kiddo. Everybody out."

I can't see the house in the dark, and I stumble as we go to the front door. She unlocks the door and reaches inside. Light floods the porch, and I step across the threshold.

"Think you'll mind this very much?" she says.

"It's . . . gorgeous," I say slowly, looking around.

I've only seen rooms like this in magazines. The furniture is white. The carpet and walls are white. Bright modern paintings hang everywhere, and her plants are so tall that most of them reach the cathedral ceiling.

Grandma St John would be furious if she ever saw this place.

"Your bedroom is down here," Aunt Leah tells me, striding off down a long dark hall, flicking light switches as she goes. The hall is lined with paintings. We turn to the right, and she opens a door. "You've got a better view of the sea here than I have in my room.

And you're right over the garden. The pool's around the other side."

The room is small, carpeted in pale blue. The spread on the single bed is brocade. The furniture is carved from a dark wood and it looks very old. A bowl of pink roses sits on the dressing table.

She shows me the loo and bathroom and turns on the little TV for me.

"I have a snack fixed for you in the kitchen. Bring it in here if you want. I'm going to change and swim for a while. You can join me, or if you're tired, I'll see you in the morning. Late in the morning."

I stand here like a lump in all this elegance, speechless and awkward. "That's fine. I'll be all right."

"Oh," she says brightly, "I know you'll be all right. But if you want something, just yell out. Okay?"

I nod, and she sweeps out, leaving a faint spicy fragrance behind to mix with the scent of the roses.

Later, after I've changed into my nightgown and robe, I go looking for her to say good night. I find the door that leads out to the pool, and I walk out on the brilliantly lighted patio. The pool ripples, blue and empty. I turn, about to go back into the house, when I hear someone sobbing.

It's Leah, sitting at the edge of the flower garden on a low stone wall. Her head is bent and her long wet hair hangs over her face. Her shoulders shake with her sobs. I return to my room.

The house is silent when I slip into my strange bed. Wide awake, I stare into the dark, wondering.

After a few minutes I hear a bird singing. The song is clear and sweet and much too brief. When he falls silent, another bird sings a different tune, and when he is through still another bird begins. One after another, all the birds in my aunt's garden sing, and when they are done I see by the bedside clock that it is four-ten.

I have been awake most of the night, listening to bird song. Now I think of my father and the bridge. I need to know why he died. Grandma and Mother did things that must have hurt him. Grandma didn't respect him, and Mother was blind to him. But I am the one who spoke killing words.

After breakfast I go outside alone and stretch out by the pool. The quiet and the sun's warmth blunt the sharp edges of my thoughts. When the pool filter kicks on and thrums faintly, the jay who has been watching me from the tall pine tree skips from one branch to another and squawks indignantly. I shift uncomfortably on the padded chaise, my sunburn sticking to the terry cloth.

My temporary peace vanishes. Through the open door, I can hear Aunt Leah talking on the phone. My mother called a few minutes ago, but she hasn't asked for me.

I hear Aunt Leah say good-bye and disappointment floods me. Well, I tell myself disgustedly, what did you expect?

"Your mother says to tell you hello," Leah says when she comes out. "She's packing up the rest of your clothes and sending them. I don't know why. You and I can pick up anything you need here. But when Silvie makes up her mind, that's it."

No kidding, I think. "What else did she say?"

"She says your grandmother is angry because you didn't stop by her apartment and say good-bye." Aunt Leah laughs sharply. "I'll bet that's not all she said. She must hate your coming here to stay with me."

Aunt Leah sits down next to me and puts a tall, greenish-looking drink on the table in front of her. "The sun is over the yardarm in Rangoon."

"What?"

She points to her drink. "It's okay to have a drink if the sun is over the yardarm. You know — the spar on a sailing ship. I figure that as long as the sun is over the yardarm somewhere, I can have a drink."

She sips the greenish stuff and smiles at me.

"How do you know if it's over the yardarm in Rangoon? Have you ever been there?"

"Probably. I've been a hell of a lot of places, kiddo. Speaking of which, where do you want to go?"

"I already am someplace I never thought I'd go," I tell her, laughing.

She waves a thin hand. "I mean, would you like to go out to dinner this evening? Or shall we go to bed early and drive to Mexico tomorrow? Or how about going to Capistrano for the day? We probably won't see any swallows, but it's beautiful. Or we can swim at —"

"Hey, hold on," I say. "You sound like a travel film. I'm not used to this place yet."

But maybe she doesn't want to sit around here with me all the time. Mother said Leah likes to travel. "If you want to, then it's fine with me," I add quickly.

She gulps half her drink and leans back in her chair. "Sorry, kiddo. I'm rushing you, I guess. I've never had a teenager staying here before, so I don't know what you like to do for amusement." She sits up, smiling. "Oh yes I do! I know just the thing. I have a friend with a son about your age, or maybe a little bit older. I'll invite them over for dinner tomorrow and maybe we can all go somewhere afterwards. Would you like that?"

Now what do I do? The last thing in this world that I want is an introduction to a boy.

"Well," I begin hesitantly, "I'm not sure about that. Not right now, anyway."

"I'm sorry, kiddo," she cries. "That was thoughtless of me. I don't know why I don't think before I talk. Of course you don't want to meet a boy yet. It's too soon. Oh dear. Forgive me and try to pretend I never said it. We'll make plans later on for you to meet him. In a couple of weeks, maybe." She finishes the rest of her drink, goes back into the house, and returns shortly with another one.

"The sun's over the yardarm in Tangier," she says.

Oh, Cameron, I think. What have I got myself into?

❈ SEVENTEEN ❈

Cameron calls me late Tuesday night. Aunt Leah hands me the phone and leaves the room.

"It's good to hear your voice," he says.

"Is something wrong?" I'm surprised that he's telephoning. We'd agreed to write to each other as often as we could, but we didn't say anything about calling.

He laughs. "Everything's wrong. You aren't here."

"I'll bet your folks don't like the idea of you calling me long distance. Or calling me short distance, either."

"They aren't home. Hey, guess what? Painters showed up at your house yesterday. It's red now and it looks good."

I feel as though a big door just slammed shut

somewhere and I'm on the wrong side of it.

"Cat? You still there?"

"I'm here," I tell him weakly.

"I went out to the farm as soon as my folks left tonight and cut the grass. And you can see where the cherries are forming. Little hard green balls. And the baby ducks are getting some of their grown-up feathers. I took pictures."

He is trying to distract me now. I guess he realizes that hearing about my house being painted shook me up.

"Did you drive my car?" I ask.

"What else? That's all right, isn't it?"

"Do your folks know?"

He laughs. "You must be kidding. No. They weren't too happy about the car. We have a sort of agreement that I won't use it until my birthday."

"Some agreement," I say, laughing. "But keep the doors locked so no one will check the mileage."

"I'm one jump ahead of you. But I'll only use it to get me to the farm once a week. Don't worry about it. What have you been doing?"

"I'm getting a tan. And yesterday we went to Mexico."

"Cat," he says, his voice serious now, "how are you getting along? I mean, *really* getting along?"

I look around the room, waiting for the furniture or the paintings or something to tell me how I'm getting along.

"I guess I'm okay. I try not to think about things

too much. Mostly I miss you, though. I think about you."

"Good. I think about you, too."

I want to ask him if he's going to the senior prom. I hope he doesn't go, but that's not fair. He's there and I'm here, and we never really talked about it anyway.

"What's new with the other kids?" I ask.

He starts to laugh. "Charlie broke off with Suzy. She says it's because his mother wouldn't let him go to Europe unless he stopped seeing her. They were going to the prom, too. Now it looks like he's going without a date."

"Poor Suzy. She saw this coming."

"Mary Beth is trying to get me to help with the decorations for the prom. I told her I'm not going and I don't care how they decorate the place. She can be a real nag when she puts her mind to it."

He's not going! I relax.

We talk for a few minutes longer, and I try to imagine what he looks like right this very moment. What is he wearing? I'd ask, but he'd think I'm silly.

"I'd better go," he says finally. "Keep writing to me every day."

"I will," I tell him. "And I use the gold pen, too. Isn't it funny that when you bought it, you thought I'd be writing to you from home and you'd be somewhere else? Everything turned out back to front."

"I miss you. Every time I look out my window, I remember that I won't be seeing you there any more. It won't be the same without my green-eyed Ms Peeping Tom."

We say good night to each other, and I sit there for a long time after we hang up. What if I never get back to Waterford? He'll get tired of writing to me and find someone else. We'll grow old without ever seeing each other again.

Aunt Leah comes into the room, carrying a thin china plate full of trifle. "See if you like this. You haven't eaten enough since you got here to keep a gnat alive. I'm beginning to think you don't like my cooking."

"I love your cooking, but I don't seem to be very hungry. Maybe it's the change in climate."

"Maybe." She sits down on the other side of the room. "And maybe not. Taste that, kiddo. It's loaded with calories."

I eat.

Aunt Leah puts on her little half-moon reading glasses and starts paging through a magazine. "Was that your boyfriend?"

Dare I call him my boyfriend? "Sort of," I hedge.

"He has a nice voice. He said his name is Cameron."

"Yes." The trifle is sticking in my throat.

She turns another page. "Is he the boy your mother was having a cow about?"

I burst out laughing and choke on the trifle. "She told you?"

"Oh, hell yes. She made it sound as though he was lurking around the shrubbery waiting for a chance to rape you." Aunt Leah smiles down at the magazine. "I had a mental picture of a mad musician leaping out of the rhododendrons every time you took out the garbage. But he sounds nice. No obscene or heavy breathing. Poor Silvie."

"Well, she has a lot of worries," I say. In spite of everything, I have to defend my mother.

"I know that. God. Your father. When she called me, I thought I was hearing things. I couldn't believe what she was saying at first. And then it hit me. Richard was free at last."

My body feels filled with cold liquid. It gushes into my stomach, and I think I'm going to throw up. Free at last? Free from what? Me? Mother? I am trying to swallow the last bite of trifle. It won't go down.

"Richard was a sensitive, gentle man." She clears her throat. "But this is a rough world. We don't have room for people like that. They get pushed out of the nest."

I swallow at last. "I don't know what you mean."

She looks up from the magazine and takes off her glasses. "You know how he was. Even when he was young he was like that. I remember him in college. He was so different from his brother. So very vulnerable. He was lucky he met Silvie, because she took good care of him."

What does she mean? My mother took care of him? My mother ignored what was wrong with him. She pretended everything was all right when it wasn't. And how does Aunt Leah know about all that anyway?

She stands up, dropping her magazine to the coffee

table. "If we're going to get an early start to the zoo, we'd better get to bed."

I carry my plate out to the kitchen and we make small talk as we close up the house for the night. My mind is spinning. When we say good night, I see that her eyes are shining with unshed tears. She mourns my father, while I still burn with guilt and anger.

Each night I lie awake until the bird chorus begins, and then, gradually, my anger disappears. I am like a muddy pond when I go to bed — terrible and unspeakable thoughts cloud my mind. Why was my father crazy? My mother said he was tired and discouraged because he lost his job. Was she willing to stand by him only when he was successful?

Grandma wanted him to be like Uncle James, but she blamed his dying on an old war. Sheila, whoever she is, didn't care enough to help him.

And I — I wanted him to be like everyone else's father and when he couldn't, I yelled at him. On his last day. That was the worst of all.

Aunt Leah sits across the table from me, sorting through the mail and sometimes sipping from a tall glass filled with ice cubes and booze. The sun is over the yardarm in Moose Jaw, she told me.

"Here's your mail from the rain country," she says as she tosses two letters to me. The first is from Cameron — I've received one from him nearly every day.

The other is from Mary Beth. She writes once or twice a week.

Once I even got a letter from my mother. Half a page and a cheque. "You passed all your exams," it said. "I had the house painted and I'm showing it as a rental until I get your father's estate settled. Have a nice time."

"I wish I'd hear from Suzy," I say. "I wrote to her twice but she hasn't answered, and I'm beginning to wonder if everything is all right."

"That's the girl who's fond of the boy with the harridan mother?" Aunt Leah crumples up an envelope and tosses it at the fireplace. She misses. "Did you ever notice that doctors' bills get home before you do?"

I laugh. "And the letters we wait for never come."

"Like the letter you're waiting for from this Suzy. Probably someone has intercepted it and sealed it up in a time capsule. You'll receive it after you and Suzy no longer even remember what it was all about. Now, if she were writing to say that Cameron has eloped with your worst enemy, that letter would come Special Delivery, brought by a man who would sing you three choruses of 'I Hope This Strikes You Blind'."

I laugh while I shake my head. "Suzy would never do anything like that."

"No. But life intervenes. It holds up our letters or sends them too soon. It tangles our speech so that the people closest to us can't understand us. And it leaves us waiting at train stations for trains that don't run any more."

Grinning, I open Cameron's letter. Aunt Leah and I

spend each afternoon like this — sitting in the dining room, going over our mail and talking. We talk about everything except my father's death and my night on the bridge. Of course, she doesn't know about the night on the bridge, but she knows that more happened than she heard from Mother, because our conversations have an awfully big hole in them. The bridge would fill it perfectly.

But I can't talk about the bridge.

I am, however, planning on asking about Sheila one of these days. I think Aunt Leah might know who she is.

One afternoon, after we'd read our mail, she talked about when she, my father, and Uncle James were in college.

"James was the most popular boy on campus and your father was always in his shadow. I never knew James to be satisfied with what he got, so he took what your father had whenever he could. Girls liked your dad, but there was only one time when the girl didn't eventually end up with James. Even I did, although I knew your father was the better man." She looked intently at me. "Do you mind hearing about this?"

I shook my head. "Go on." Next she's going to tell about Sheila, I thought. Sheila was the one who wouldn't leave my father for Uncle James.

She shrugged and laughed. "No, I think you've heard enough about ancient times."

"I'd like to hear more," I urged. "Did you and my dad go out for very long?"

"Not very long. Then James smiled at me and I followed. To my inevitable sorrow." She bit her lip and I waited. But she got up then and busied herself with dinner preparations.

Maybe Sheila happened to my father between the time he dated Aunt Leah and the day he met Mother.

Aunt Leah turns the pages of a magazine, exclaiming over the ads.

I interrupt. "Do you remember who my dad dated after you started going out with Uncle James?"

She looks up at me, surprised. "For heaven's sake. What brought that up?"

Prentending I don't really care isn't easy. "I just wondered. It's interesting, hearing about how things used to be."

"Don't get the idea that your father was fretting over my dating his brother. He always considered me just a good friend."

"I guess. But he must have started taking out someone else. Did you know her?"

Leah frowns, concentrating. "That was so long ago. Let's see. I remember the night James gave a party — a picnic, really — at the farm. Everybody was there. What a mob! We ate by the pond and danced under the trees. I don't think your father had a special date that night. He might have, but it wouldn't have mattered

168

because that's the night he met your mother. I'll never forget that as long as I live. I thought James was going after her — well, he did! I was so jealous I made myself sick. But after that your father started taking your mother out, and as far as I know, he never even looked at anyone else. Why are you so curious?"

"He could have taken out someone else. He didn't marry Mother until he came back from the war. That was a couple of years later, at least."

She looked at me curiously. "What is it that you're not asking? I have a hunch you're after a very special answer."

I can't tell her about my dad writing to Sheila and calling me by her name. But I can't bear knowing that he cared about another woman more than he did my mother.

And I accused him of it. He died thinking that I knew about Sheila.

I read Cameron's letter over again to assure myself that he's still in the world. I need to talk to him, really talk.

The kids in his class will be going to their prom tonight. His letter tells me that he's going out to dinner with his parents and grandparents. If I were there . . .

Next year I'll take Cameron to my senior prom. If I get to go home. I write to Mom and ask her how long I'm supposed to stay, but she doesn't answer. When I call there, she's never home. And today Aunt Leah drove me by the high school the kids in this neighbourhood attend.

The truth about Sheila is only one of the things I'm afraid to learn.

As I'm tearing open Mary Beth's letter, I notice how awful her handwriting is getting. She hasn't been having a very good time these past weeks. The job is wearing her out, and last I heard, she still didn't have a date for the prom.

"I hate this town," her letter begins. "First of all, I'm missing you. Second, I'm getting a D in biology and my mother is planning on having me locked up in a tower in the woods where I'll have nothing but bread and water to eat until I'm old enough to vote. Which is fine since I don't have a prom date.

"Listen, Cat, this will crack you up. The manager at work told me she's been trying to get in touch with you but no one ever answers the phone. She wants to hire you! Can you believe it? I didn't tell her you were in California. I just said I'd let you know and if you weren't busy, maybe you'd get in touch. I can just see you rushing back to go to work in good old Grease Grotto.

"I wouldn't blame you if you never came back. It rained three times this week even though summer is practically here.

"Cameron looks like he lost his last friend. Are you writing to him?

"Charlie crashed his car the night before last. Everyone says he was drunk and Suzy thinks he did it on purpose. Don't worry about him — he's going to be okay as soon as he gets the cast off his arm, but his car was a write-off. What a jerk. I'll never know what Suzy sees in him. I think they're planning on running away together — but not until he gets back from Europe, of course.

"Cat, we weren't going to tell you this, but I decided I ought to. I thought maybe you'd like knowing about it. On the night your father had been gone for four weeks, Cameron and Suzy and I dropped a lot of wildflowers over the bridge and Suzy and I said this little prayer we wrote. We picked the flowers out at your farm by the pond. I hope we did what you would have wanted.

"I love you, little pal."

I think she has killed me. I bend my head over the letter, gasping from the hurt. My eyes are on fire.

Aunt Leah takes the letter out of my stiff fingers and reads it. I hear her catch her breath.

"Cat?"

"I'm okay."

But she isn't worried about me. I look up and see her leaning against the table.

"Did your father . . . Was it the bridge on the road to the farm?"

"Yes."

"I had hoped it wasn't. Not that bridge."

I sit up straight and take the letter from her hand. "One bridge is the same as another," I lie.

She's not listening. "Once, when he was driving me out to the farm for dinner, he stopped and asked me to look over the railing. There was a cave down there, washed out of the cliff by the river. He said —"

"That's where the fairies and shooting stars and talking caterpillars are born," I finish. My mouth is dry.

We don't look at each other. I fold up the letter and put it back in the envelope. Through the open door I hear the pool filter click on again. The garden jay protests.

My father told Aunt Leah about the cave. But it was a private, secret thing.

"You never cry, do you, kiddo?" she asks suddenly.

I look up at her then. Her eyes are rimmed with tears, and they spill over and run down her face.

"No. Not even that night. Not even when they found him down there. Not even when my mother told me I was coming here to stay with you and I wasn't used to him being gone yet."

She doesn't wipe her tears away. They drip off her chin. "You were there that night? You saw him?"

I shake my head. "He'd already done it — gone off the bridge — when Cameron and I drove by and saw his car. But we were there when they found him. It was my birthday."

She doesn't say anything for a long, long time. Then she wipes her face on the backs of her hands. "He wouldn't have thought of that, you know. When he got really bad, he never knew what day it was. Or even what year it was. He mixed up people. He would never have deliberately hurt you that way."

Oh yes he would, I think. I'd found out about Sheila.

"I suppose not," I say.

She looks around the room, as if she just realized it was there. "Gee, kiddo, I'd better do something about dinner."

I watch her while she pulls vegetables out of the refrigerator. She is trying to distract herself. I'm not the only one who doesn't want to think about the bridge.

"How do you know so much about my father's problem?" I ask calmly.

She looks up at me while she washes lettuce at the sink. "Why, I was still in Waterford when your father went to the hospital that first time. Right after your parents were married."

❖ EIGHTEEN ❖

I lie awake listening to the birds sing, but the muddy pool in my mind will not clear. Hour after hour I've been lying here, hating her, hating them all. But most of all Aunt Leah.

Because I wanted to love her. I came here scared to death because my father was dead and my mother had all but told me she didn't want me around. Cameron was just the excuse she used. And Aunt Leah gave me a place to sleep and fed me and took me everywhere with her, even to luncheons and dinners with her friends.

But she is the cause of it all. She and I. We killed him — she because he couldn't have her and I because when he needed me, I turned on him.

Leah. Sheila. Leah. Sheila. He never could keep

names straight. Aunt Leah is the Sheila he wrote to. It was her picture he was looking at that day.

What did she do with his letter? Throw it away like her doctor's bill?

She wanted Uncle James and my father turned to my mother.

My sheets are tangled around my legs, and my bedroom is like an oven. I am burning up with hating the women in my father's life. All of us.

I get up. In the dark, I find the door to the patio and I slip outside.

The night smells of gardenias. The flowers gleam along the rock wall, and I sit near them. Overhead a bird cries mournfully, alone in the magnolia tree.

"He's wonderful, isn't he?"

I hold my breath. Aunt Leah is sitting on the steps going down to the pool. She raises her glass to me. "The sun's over the yardarm in Bora Bora."

I turn my head away. "You drink too much."

Silence. Another bird sings from the same tree.

"You're angry with me, aren't you?" Aunt Leah says. "You didn't like what I told you about your father. I don't understand why they didn't tell you a long time ago. It was nothing to be ashamed of — but your father was always ashamed."

I hug my knees and look across the pool, into the dark. "Waterford is a small town. Maybe that's why they didn't want to talk about it."

"But they should have told you."

"Well, they didn't."

I stand up suddenly. I wanted to be alone, but Aunt Leah seems to be set out here for the night — she has a bottle next to her, as well as the silver ice bucket. Drunk, but with lots of style.

"I wish you'd stay for a while. Please."

I sit down again, feeling foolish. In spite of everything, I still want to like her.

I have to have somebody.

"That first time was the worst," she said. "He was in the hospital for two months. The next time wasn't so bad. It was just for a few days. They were developing new kinds of medication then, and he seemed to get better."

"You told me that before we went to bed."

"I know. I guess I wanted to hear it again myself. When James died, I didn't hesitate to move here because I was sure your father was going to be all right. Well, as all right as someone like him can ever be in a world like this. And your mother had always coped so well. Better than I could have. She was never afraid. She just — kept going."

"Not this last time."

She pours another drink. "Her letters never even hinted that he was getting worse."

"He stopped taking his pills. I found bottles of them in his desk. Or maybe he forgot. I didn't know about the pills until after he died or I could have reminded him. She didn't."

Ice clinks and the bird suddenly stops singing. "How do you know that? Maybe she did and he ignored her."

I shrug in the dark. The bird is still silent and I'm sorry. That one didn't get a chance to finish his song.

"Grandma said it was the war that made him do it."

"Grandma would say something like that. She knows better. The war certainly didn't do him any good, but he was already fragile. James knew it. He often took advantage of it. And so did their mother. But never Silvie."

I don't know what to say. I remember the times since January when I tried to get my mother to admit that Dad needed some kind of help, but all she would say was that he was tired — or discouraged about being out of work. Never, not once, did she let on that my father had been under treatment for serious emotional problems or that he had been in mental hospitals when I was too young to know what was happening.

And then, of course, there had been the business of Sheila the Mysterious Woman from My Father's Past. Secrets. I guess we've all got a few.

"I wish the birds would start singing again."

Aunt Leah laughs. "It's only one bird, a mockingbird. Didn't you know that?"

"One bird? Are you sure?"

Clink goes the ice again. "He's an old friend. But he wants me to think that he's several old friends, so that's why he sings several songs. When the baby birds are big enough and he doesn't have to worry any more, he'll just use his own song."

I'm disappointed. I rest my head on my knees again, thinking about the bird in the tree.

"Parents do some pretty strange things to protect their children, kiddo."

"I guess."

After a while I go back to bed, leaving Aunt Leah in the dark. The sun's over the yardarm in Portofino.

At noon the next day Aunt Leah says, "Let's give a party."

I'm barely awake, but she looks like a model in a fashion magazine, and she's rushing around the house plumping cushions and blowing specks of invisible dust off mirrors. The housekeeper was here yesterday — everything is perfect. But she keeps on fussing.

"What sort of party?" I poke at my melon and wish she'd go downtown or over to see a friend. I want to be alone.

"A big one. Tomorrow night. I'll invite everyone I can think of, even that boy you don't want to meet. You'll need someone your own age to dance with."

She's as excited as Mary Beth gets over a party. I try to imagine her dancing under the cherry trees in the orchard and I can't. She's wearing a designer dress that probably cost more than my whole wardrobe for a whole year.

"I'll get busy on the phone and start inviting people, and you think of what you'd like to eat. I'll need to tell the caterer what to fix."

I shrug and poke my melon again. "I don't care. Anything is fine."

If she hears me she doesn't let on. She's still smiling as she runs out of the room.

She doesn't slow down until dinner. "Sorry about today, kiddo. You must have been bored. We'll try to get out for a little while tomorrow, but I've got a lot to do before the party."

"It doesn't matter," I say. I almost called her Sheila.

I spend the evening watching television in my room, wishing I had enough courage to call Cameron. But what would I say if one of his parents answered? They probably wouldn't like it.

At ten o'clock, just because I really need someone to talk to, I call my mother again, and for the first time she's home. Not that I've been trying very hard to reach her.

I'm almost embarrassed to speak to her because it's been so long. "How is everything going?" I say.

"Not too bad," she tells me. "Is everything all right there? I didn't expect anyone to be calling so late."

"You're never home. I've tried calling at all hours, but you're always gone. And you don't answer letters." I'm sounding like a spoiled little kid, I know. But I am her daughter and my father died, and you'd think she would have cared enough to talk to me.

"I've been terribly busy, Catherine," she tells me wearily. "You have no idea how much work I've had to do around here to get the place ready to rent. And I've been swamped at the office, too. But the money is coming in, so I'll be able to get rid of some of the debts that were worrying me."

"So you don't have to sell the house?" I ask quickly.

"Catherine, we've been all over that. I must sell it. There is no other way. But I think this one family may be interested in renting until it's available for sale and then buying it."

"But is there any chance you won't have to sell? Couldn't you just rent it for a while until things get better?"

She sighs, letting me know I'm impossible and she's tired and this whole conversation is a mistake. "Catherine, I'm seriously considering an apartment on Darrow Street, in that new building overlooking the park. In fact, I was thinking of going over there again tomorrow."

I want to ask her if the apartment has a bedroom for me, but I don't.

"I hope you're adjusting to the climate there," she says, smoothly changing subjects. "Grandma St John says she always gets hay fever in California."

"I'm just fine, Mother."

"She says that I shouldn't have let you go, but I'm glad you're there. The weather is so nice and you have a chance to rest. Leah may not be everyone's cup of tea, but she's not going to neglect you. She hasn't been, has she?"

"Of course not. She takes me everywhere with her, even to her club for lunch. I'm learning to play golf."

"There, see? Isn't that nice? And you didn't want to go. Aren't you glad you did?"

She doesn't want me back. "Mother, when can I come home?"

I listen to her breathe. "Oh, Catherine, you're not going to start off about that again, are you? I told you, you'll be spending the summer there. Leah and I have it all worked out."

I know that when I start to talk my voice will be shaking, but I have to say something. I must.

"Sometimes I wonder what you *really* think about what's happened, Mother. Everything you say is so . . . *planned*. Is it all lies?"

"Catherine, you're upset. We'll take this up another time. Now you go to bed and get a good night's rest. And I'll call you as soon as I have a free moment."

"All right, Mother."

"And don't make Leah sorry she invited you."

"Good night, Mother."

The next night Aunt Leah's party spills out of the house across the garden and patio. She glitters and shimmers, moving from one person to another, drink in hand. They love her. I sit like a lump in a new dress, watching soberly and thinking about Cameron's last letter. He misses me, he said, and his parents are sending him to summer music camp for the first two weeks of July. "They can't stand me moping around any more," he wrote. "But don't worry about the farm. I'll find someone to cut the grass and pick the cherries."

I want to go home to cut the grass and pick the cherries at my farm. But I'm here, and I must make an effort for my aunt's sake.

"Just say hello to the people you've met and tell the others who you are," she told me earlier. "Don't be nervous."

I wasn't nervous — I just wasn't in the mood for a party.

The boy she invited so I'd have someone to dance with is here, gawping at me across the patio. He's cute — but he isn't Cameron.

Candles float on the pool, each one in a small glass bubble. Paper lanterns hang from the trees, and I wonder what the jay and the mockingbird think of all this.

"Do you mind having some company?" the boy asks as he sits down next to me without waiting to be asked. His name is Craig.

"Have you had something to eat?" I ask brightly.

"I've already been through the line twice," he says, laughing at himself. "Would you like to dance?"

"Why don't we just sit here and talk," I suggest slyly. "Tell me about yourself."

I can't dance with him, because he isn't Cameron and this isn't the orchard. And the last time I danced was the night my father died.

"Don't you like to dance?" he asks.

"No. Where do you go to school?"

He tells me more than I really wanted to know about him, but I see Aunt Leah glancing at us from time to time, so I want her to think I'm having a good time.

After a while the candles sputter out, and the guests go inside. The boy excuses himself, having given up on me, and I sit in the pale light of a peach-coloured paper lantern, waiting. When the music stops, I go in and stand with my aunt while the guests leave.

"Did you have a good time, kiddo?" she asks. She drains her drink and hands the glass to one of the maids.

"It was a beautiful party," I tell her truthfully. "Everyone was so glamorous."

She looks at me carefully. "They're just people, Cat. Good old friends."

Then she hugs me suddenly, as if she is worried about me. "You're so thin. Why are you scaring me so much?"

"What do you mean, scaring you?" Now she is scaring me.

"You're so good and so quiet. Aren't teenagers supposed to be noisy and moody and spoiled?"

I shrug. I don't know what teenagers are supposed to be like any more. Maybe I never did.

She kisses me on my forehead. "Go to bed now, kiddo. You must be exhausted."

I go to bed, but I can't sleep. I hear the maids and the housekeeper leave, and finally Aunt Leah's bedroom door closes. The night is over.

How lonely she is, I think. The guests leave and she is all alone again. Now she doesn't even have the satisfaction of knowing that my father is fifteen hundred miles away and she could telephone him if she really wanted to. There won't be any more letters, not even the crazy ones.

Who has lost the most?

The mockingbird sings only one song tonight. I guess he's worn out, too.

❖ NINETEEN ❖

I have accumulated a shoe box full of letters since I've been here. Most are from Cameron and Mary Beth, but some of the thickest ones are from Suzy. Charlie is in Europe now, and her heart has broken into one zillion pieces, she says. She wrote to me that she and Charlie were thinking of running away together when he got back, but he decided against it because he was sure his parents would cancel his credit cards.

My mother has even written to me since my phone call. She rented the house and moved into the apartment she liked. It has a bedroom for me, but she hasn't asked me to come home. She is very tired, she says, and business is keeping her on the go all the time. And she told me she was sorry that she hadn't written to me when I first came here, but she was having "a difficult time adjusting."

So was I.

Grandma wrote to me twice, once to tell me to keep an eye on Leah because she wasn't to be trusted and once to warn me that Leah would probably corrupt me by exposing me to "wild people like artists and musicians, although I suppose you're used to people like that since you were hanging around with that Cameron who is going to music school, I hear. Dead in the gutter before he's twenty-one, you just wait."

Last week I sent Cameron a wonderful seashell for his birthday. He's leaving for music camp today, according to his letters.

"I'll write to you every day or maybe even twice a day, since I expect to be bored out of my skull. The only other person I'll know there is Martie Crossmyer, the tuba player from school. This is an outdoor music camp, so I'll think about you when I'm pouring water out of my guitar. How's that suntan coming along? I wish I could see it."

I hold the letter to my lips before I put it away. Some of his letters are worn out because I've read them so much.

Every night before she goes to bed, Aunt Leah swims in the pool. Tonight I decide to go in with her, and together we lap the pool until we are both exhausted. We don't talk much any more. A thick silence has built up between us — or rather, I have built it and she doesn't understand why.

She climbs out of the water and wraps herself in a huge towel. "Better get out now," she calls to me. "I don't want you swimming alone."

As I push myself through the water towards the tile steps, I hear the front doorbell echoing.

"Who can that be at this hour? Come on, Cat. Out of the water."

She runs across the patio towards the house as the bell chimes again. "I'm coming, I'm coming!" she shouts. As I climb out of the pool, water beads on my arms, raising gooseflesh. A light cool wind rattles the leaves of the magnolia tree. I sling my towel over my shoulder and start for the house just as Aunt Leah appears in the lighted doorway.

"Cat," she calls out. "You'd better come inside."

"Coming."

She stands there outlined by light, and I can't see her face but I know she's excited. "What's going on?"

"You'll see. Come inside."

I don't believe what I see. He is standing awkwardly in the hall, with his guitar case and a blue nylon suitcase at his feet. He smiles and shrugs self-consciously. "Here I am, at music camp."

"Cameron!" I cry, throwing my arms around him.

He hugs me, looking over my head at the doorway where my aunt is standing. "Hey, you're all wet," he says. Then he blurts, "Aw, heck," and kisses me once, hard and briefly.

"Is there something I should know?" Aunt Leah says. "Should someone know where you are or have you run away?"

"I'm supposed to be at music camp," he says, grinning at me. "My folks drove me there this morning and I left right after they did. I hitched a ride to the airport and here I am."

"They'll kill you when they find out," I say.

"They won't find out. I gave Martie postcards to mail for me every other day."

"Oh, dear," Aunt Leah murmurs. "Oh, hell. I have a feeling I'm going to be in trouble. I *know* I'm going to be in trouble. Look, kids, this is all very romantic, but it just won't do. You see that, don't you?"

Cameron shifts his feet uncomfortably. "I wasn't going to ask you if I could stay here. I brought enough money with me to stay in a cheap motel. Don't worry — I'll manage. You won't get into trouble, I promise."

"Ha. How old are you? Seventeen? Eighteen? Oh, God, not eighteen. We'll really be in for it if you're of legal age and chasing after a teenager."

"He's sixteen," I say. I turn to Cameron. "Where did you get all that money?"

"Birthday money. And my savings. And I sold my bike."

"My mother will kill you if your folks don't," I say. "But you're here now, so you might as well sit down. We'll think of what to do later. I'm going to get dressed."

I hurry off to my room. Behind me I can hear Aunt

188

Leah fussing at Cameron, but she doesn't really sound angry. Just afraid.

Oh, Cameron. If our folks find out, they'll never let us see each other again. Why did you do it?

But I'm so glad you came! I'm so very, very glad.

While I'm changing into jeans and a thin cotton shirt, I can hear voices from the living room. I'm so nervous that I'm trembling inside my skin.

When I join them, Cameron is sitting on the white sofa, eating potato chips and drinking pop, and he looks as relaxed as he does in his own room. Aunt Leah raises her glass.

"Sun's over the yardarm in Maracaibo," she says, and Cameron bursts out laughing.

"What did you decide?" I ask. Am I the only one worrying?

"Cameron can stay here in the little room over the garage, but only for a few days. We've agreed that he ought to go back for at least part of the session at the music camp," Aunt Leah says, and Cameron nods his head.

"But how will he explain where he's been?"

"If the worst happens, we'll tell the truth," Aunt Leah says smugly, and I think that of the three of us, she is the least practical. What sounds like simple truth to one person is a mixed-up horror story to someone else. I tell them that, but they don't seem to care. So I add this problem to the rest of the problems I'm trying not to care about.

"I'll let you show Cameron around town tomorrow," Aunt Leah tells me. "I'm worn out with all this excitement."

I doubt it, but she yawns to convince Cameron and goes off to bed.

We sit and look at each other.

"Well, what do you think?" he says at last.

I can't help grinning. "I think we are making an awful mistake, but right now I don't want to care."

We talk for half an hour, and then I show Cameron the stairs to the cluttered little room over the garage. I guess we're embarrassed — we shake hands good night, laugh, and I run away before I blush.

The next day I take Cameron to an outdoor restaurant for lunch, and then we walk through a park while we talk.

"Aren't you and your aunt getting along?"

I'm busy looking at him, caring too much again and soaking up his smile so that I can remember it for the rest of my life. His question surprises me. "What gave you that idea?"

He shrugs and catches my hand, squeezing it. "She tries too hard to please you, I guess. And you try too hard to be polite. What happened?"

I look away from him. "She told me that my father had been in a mental hospital. More than once, when I was too little to remember. She acts as if that explains everything."

"Maybe it does."

"You know better than that."

He stops beside a bench and pulls me down on it. "I

know what you're thinking. You think that what he did was your fault, because you got mad at him when he didn't show up to take you for your driving test. But nobody kills himself because of one little blow-up. He'd been sick for a long time. He got tired out."

"Cameron Fairchild, the world-famous psychiatrist," I mutter. Can't he see that someone is responsible for what happened? "It's a lot more complicated than you think."

"Then tell me what makes it complicated. Your dad was sick, so he did what sick people do sometimes. It was his decision."

"You're making it sound as if he just decided to do it and did it. Like going to the store for a loaf of bread."

He slides his arm around me and pulls my head against his shoulder. "What were you supposed to do to stop him?"

I turn my face against his shirt. "I don't know. If someone had told me that he'd been in the hospital, I wouldn't have let myself get angry with him. I'd have thought of a way to help."

"No one else was able to help."

"No one else was trying any more! Grandma wouldn't even admit the truth to herself. And Mother did such a good job of hiding it from me that she couldn't see it herself."

I look out across the park. Three kids are flying a red kite. It twists and struggles in the wind.

"Maybe she thought she was protecting you," he says.

I sit up straight. "And maybe she knew that if she told me, she'd have to give up cleaning the house every five minutes and do something for Dad." I know he's right, but if I give up being angry with myself because I yelled at my father and then give up being angry with Mother because she was trying to protect me, who can I blame?

The kids have let out the string too far. The kite is only a red dot high above us now, jerking frantically against the sweep of windblown blue sky as if it wants to escape.

"If everyone had been honest," I say, "and if I'd tried harder to understand him, and if *she* hadn't been on his mind all the time, then my father would still be alive."

"Who's *she*? You mean your mother?"

"I mean Aunt Leah. She's the one I told you about. Sheila."

Cameron stares at me. "Sheila? But her name is Leah. Why would he call her Sheila?"

"Because he mixed up names all the time. You know how he was. Leah. Sheila. You can see how he might do it."

Cameron shakes his head. "Not any more than I can see how he'd mix up Sheila with Silvie. How do you know he wasn't talking about your mother?"

"He wrote a letter to Sheila. Why would he write to my mother? He could have talked to her any time."

But even while I'm speaking I see what's wrong with my idea. He was too tired to talk about trouble.

He just wanted the farm and the cherry trees. Peaceful things.

And maybe Mother hadn't been able to talk, either. Maybe she was worn out from caring and could only keep on keeping on.

"Why don't you ask your aunt about Sheila?" Cameron says. "There could be a simple explanation."

"Don't push me."

"Maybe you don't want to know."

"So maybe I don't. What difference would it make now? My father is dead."

"Maybe there never was a Sheila except in his mind."

I consider this. Maybe Sheila is like the fairies and shooting stars and talking caterpillars. Magic.

We are silent now, each of us wrapped up in questions that either don't have answers or shouldn't be answered. I'm not sure I know the difference.

The kite string breaks. The kids run across the acres of grass, reaching and shouting, but the kite flashes away, higher and higher until it disappears.

"It got away," I say sadly as the kids wander off, heads down, feet scuffing the grass.

"They shouldn't have let it fly so high," Cameron grumbles. "That was dumb."

"They didn't expect the string to break." Neither did we.

We stand up and stretch. The warm wind tousles my short hair and flutters Cameron's shirt collar. "I know where we can get the best chocolate ice cream in the whole world," I tell him. "Do you want to try it?"

"Sounds good." He takes my hand again, and we walk towards the street. "What do you think you'll do?"

"About what?"

"Are you going to ask your aunt if she's Sheila?"

"You don't let up, do you?"

"You'd know for certain."

I shake my head. "I guess I don't really want to know who danced in the orchard first."

Cameron starts to laugh. "That's right! The April dancers!" He grabs my other hand and swings me around on the grass. "We'll do it again, Cat. Next year in April, when the cherry blossoms fall. We will, won't we?"

"Yes!" I shout. "Yes, and every year after that."

He hugs me then, so hard that I think my ribs will crack. "We don't have to be like the rest of them, Green Eyes. We'll always talk. We'll always listen."

But I know better. Maybe the best thing we'll ever be able to do is try.

❈ TWENTY ❈

Cameron stayed four days and then decided to check in at the music camp. "I saw what I needed to see," he tells me late on the last night, when we are sitting on the patio. "You're all right. I can wait until you come back now." .

"Maybe I won't be coming back. What if my mother is trying to dump me on Aunt Leah?"

"Maybe she's having a harder time getting along than she lets on. She might not want you to see her like that."

I'm about to say that if that's how she really feels, why doesn't she say so, but I don't. Mother isn't ready to give up thinking of me as a baby.

We take Cameron to the airport, and Aunt Leah

discreetly pops into the coffee shop to let me say good-bye to him.

"Your new apartment isn't very far from my house," he tells me. "I've already checked it out."

"But it's a long way from Seattle."

"It's not so far. I'll be home at weekends, I promise."

"But what if your folks find out you were here and get mad? They might not let you see me."

"Cat, I'm old enough to be in college! If they find out, I'll tell them I took off because they were so pig-headed. But I came back on my own because I'm not pig-headed. It's not as if I broke any laws. They'll get over it."

"That's not much of an explanation."

"Not everything has a perfect explanation. You ought to know that by now."

We watch at the windows, our arms around each other. His plane is here now, on time but too soon. "Write to me from camp," I remind him.

"Are you going to talk to your mother about going home?"

"Maybe I'll just go home. What can she do about it?"

He laughs, looking down at me, dazzling me again. "Right," he says. "After all, if she didn't let you in, what would the neighbours say?"

He's gone, with a backward look and a wave, and I have to sit down because his going weakens me.

Aunt Leah finds me a few minutes later.

"Let's go out for a real breakfast, kiddo. I'm starving. And as soon as the shops open, let's look around for a few new things for ourselves."

I want to hug her. Her smooth tanned face looks so young, but her eyes hold a knowing of that lost place where the dark is born, and there's no one to keep it away from her.

"That sounds good to me. But you know what I want most of all? I want a big red kite and lots of string. Then let's go to the park where the kids fly their kites."

"Oh, God," she groans. "You'll be the absolute death of me. But maybe I can get through it if I have a new skirt and one of those striped silk blouses I was looking at the other day. And of course, the sun will be over the yardarm in Monte Carlo."

Later I am trying on a new swimsuit in my bedroom after dinner when I hear Aunt Leah answer the telephone.

"Silvie," she cries, "what is the matter?"

Holding my breath, I open my door. "Well, of course he was here," Aunt Leah says, her voice crackling with outraged innocence. "You don't think I would have let him stay in a motel, do you? He stayed in the little studio apartment over the garage, swam in my pool a few times, and went to the park with Cat. We sent him off this morning to his summer camp."

I creep down the hall until I'm standing next to Aunt Leah. My heart is hammering.

Aunt Leah listens with a peculiar expression on her face, opens her mouth several times, and shuts it again.

When my mother is worked up, it's hard to interrupt her.

Finally Aunt Leah gets her turn. "Well, I'm sorry they were worried, but after all, he left almost as soon as he got here, and he's certainly old enough to make his own travel arrangements and explanations. I'm sure he's at that camp by now, which they could have found out for themselves if they'd just called the place back. What a fuss! No wonder teenagers are so odd. Silvie, I'd like to remind you that you weren't much older when you went to London for a summer with that silly nincompoop Mavis Ketchplatt and both of you caught some sort of horrible skin disease, or maybe it was athlete's foot, when you tried to save money by staying in a simply awful old shack. Cameron was sleeping in an immaculate bed, and I can assure you that the pool is cleaner than drinking water."

Aunt Leah has won the battle. I'm certain Mother is in shock from that tirade. I lean against the wall and let out the breath I was holding. Aunt Leah winks at me and hands me the phone.

"Your mother would like to talk to you."

"Catherine, what is going on?" Mother starts off, but she is definitely out of steam.

"I don't really know. Cameron just showed up here and left again. I guess he didn't want to go to that music camp, but he decided he'd better. Or maybe Aunt Leah and I bored him to death. Mostly we just go shopping and to museums, you know." I wink back at Aunt Leah.

Mother sighs. She's very good at sighing. "The

Fairchilds are worried sick. They didn't find out until yesterday that Cameron wasn't at the camp, and they've been calling everywhere. It finally occurred to me that perhaps he ran away to you."

"Oh, Mother, please," I scoff.

"But what am I going to tell them?" she asks. "This is terrible!"

"Why don't you let Cameron explain everything to them? It's not really our business. I mean, what are they going to think if you start telling them what their son is doing? It's his problem, not yours. You'd only embarrass them."

"That's right," she says slowly, and I know her little polished wheels are turning. "If they can't keep an eye on him, why should I? I can't be expected to do everything."

"And after all, we do owe Cameron something," I add hastily. "He arranged for kids to pick the cherries, and when he was here he told me that he sold the crop to the Old Country Garden store just before he left. I would have forgotten all about it and so did you, I bet. We can use the money to pay off some of the bills, right?"

"Hmm."

"Mother," I say firmly, "I'm coming back in two weeks because I'll need the time to get ready for school. I hope my room is ready."

"Oh, Catherine, your room will be just lovely." I hear the surprise in her voice. Does she understand that I have taken responsibility for my life? Not yet, perhaps.

She goes on and on about tidying and cleaning the apartment. But then, Mother was always fussy about that sort of thing. It's one way of making sure that at least part of the day turns out right. And it beats going crazy.

When we hang up, Aunt Leah asks, "Is it going to be all right, kiddo?" Her eyes are shut, as if she's afraid to look at me.

"It's going to be fine. I guess you heard me say that I'm going home in two weeks."

She looks at me then. "I'll miss you, Cat."

"I'll be back, wait and see." I walk into the living room and turn around in front of her. "What do you think of this swimsuit? Did I pick the right one?"

"It's perfect," she says, distracted from her worries now. "I think you might even have gained a pound or two. Now let's have our swim early tonight and watch a late movie. And tomorrow we'll drop down to Mexico again. I've been thinking about that wonderful aquamarine ring we saw there. You should have it. And we'll pick up a few odds and ends for your friends."

That beats going crazy, too, I think. Shopping can be like a ceremony.

I had a ceremony of my own today. I deliberately cut my red kite loose this afternoon. I watched it until it soared away, and then I cried. It's so hard to let go and say good-bye.

"But I'll get you another kite," Aunt Leah cried. "Are you sure you're all right?"

"No, but I'm trying," I told her as I blew my nose.

DEAR SHEILA

Cameron and I went to the bridge today. We brought fireweed and daisies, the last of the summer flowers blooming at the farm. After we dropped them over the railings, I cried for a long time. I'm not sure all of my tears were for my father. Maybe some of them were for the St John women. We did the best we could, and maybe if we remember that, we can forgive each other. Sometimes the kite gets away.

Sincerely,

CATHERINE SILVIE ST JOHN